THE MYTHOLOGY, THE METAL *and* THE HOURGLASS

JOURNEY THROUGH THE EYE OF THE NEEDLE

First Was the Word.
Then Came the Story.
Fantasy Returns to Reality.
A Journey through the Eye of the Needle Has a Point of No Return.

JONATHAN HAMMOCK

WESTBOW
P R E S S®
A DIVISION OF THOMAS NELSON
& ZONDERVAN

Scripture taken from the King James Version of the Bible.

WestBow Press books may be ordered through booksellers or by contacting:

WestBow Press
A Division of Thomas Nelson & Zondervan
1663 Liberty Drive
Bloomington, IN 47403
www.westbowpress.com
1 (866) 928-1240

ISBN: 978-1-5127-1217-9 (sc)
ISBN: 978-1-5127-1221-6 (hc)
ISBN: 978-1-5127-1218-6 (e)

Library of Congress Control Number: 2015914910

Print information available on the last page.

WestBow Press rev. date: 09/23/2015

Written for a day of reconciliation,
In memory of my father.

CONTENTS

Part I   The Hammer

Part II   The Chain

Part III The Sword

Part IV The Bell

PREFACE

There is not much I like to share about myself. I would rather write about the life my father lived. It would be more interesting than anything that I have done. James Gramling Hammock was a preacher and is currently in a place that his soul will flourish forever. It is a place his body could not go due to a fatal accident involved on a highway. He hit some black ice in the middle of December while driving a van. A semi-truck was struck causing him to lose his life while in the emergency room. He was traveling to Columbia, Missouri to visit a member of his church who themselves was in the hospital for different reasons.

My dad lived a life of service. Before getting the call to preach, he had served in the army in the 1970s. He was part of an airborne division and was ready to be dropped out of a plane by parachute, if the need arose. Fortunately, he served in peacetime.

Shortly before my birth in 1982, my father pastored his first church, in Calahan, Florida. He saw it as his purpose to help build up small churches. Whenever a church would grow to a certain point, he would leave for a new ministry. Our family would go wherever that might be.

Little of interest happened to me during my early years, unless you count speaking my first word or learning to crawl. Not long after I started to walk, I broke my leg while climbing onto a gravestone. For some reason, I thought cemeteries were fun places to play.

Our second church was in Taft, Florida, where I began kindergarten. We moved to another church after a couple of years there. We never complained about heading for another place. I was excited about traveling to a new home. We didn't miss our former town until we had reached a new locale.

The place I miss the most is Roddy, a small spot in Georgia. It barely qualified as a town. It had only a gas station, a church, and a few scattered farm homes. We spent four unforgettable years in this wonderful place. I had never felt such freedom before and have never felt it since. Some of my best friends lived here. We built forts in trees and lived out the mischief found in the pages of a Mark Twain novel. The area had endless dirt roads where we could get lost, and one time my sister and I did. We were riding our bicycles and became too confident that we knew where we were going. We eventually found our way back but not until after nightfall. Our parents had been very worried and were relieved when we returned, though they were angry with us.

I felt a sense of adventure during these years, and this would sow the seeds for many choices in my life, some good and some bad. I made one crucial decision. My father led me to the Lord, and I became saved. I don't remember the exact age when I was born again, but I recall walking down the aisle toward my dad, who stood at the altar. He led me in the sinner's prayer, and I asked Jesus to live within me and to be my Savior.

I had learned early in life how the world began, but during this time I began to ponder how it would end. I was taught about the apocalypse at a young age, and these lessons changed me. Seeing the sky above open fields and dirt roads made me consider the bigger picture.

I didn't have a clue what I was going to do with my life. I had little ambition and was content to remain a preacher's kid for the rest of my life. This attitude would lead me to bad decisions. I would coast through life, holding my breath until I got to heaven. This seemed like a good idea at the time.

This was the way I lived growing up in Missouri. I glided through middle school and high school without a care and got average grades with little effort. I have had many hobbies throughout the years, from playing the trombone to acting, but none completely stuck with me.

I was proud of some activities. I loved being part of a youth group in Clinton, Missouri, led by Joey Conway, a person who has had a big impact on many young people's lives. He is still in Clinton, leading a strong church with a rich future. Northeast Baptist has made quite an investment in young people.

It wasn't until the passing of my father during my first year at college that I realized my plan for living wouldn't work. I could no longer live vicariously through my dad. It was time for me to fulfill the commitments I made to God long before in a small corner in Georgia, but I was not ready to do this. I found that getting even average grades required more effort than I was willing to give, so I blew off college.

I changed my career path many times but eventually decided to cling to low- paying jobs. This was an important step for me, however. I had to get real with my life, and I gained a better work ethic during this time. Some say that no one changes, but there were definite changes going on in me. As the song says, once I was blind, but now I see. Once I was a quitter, but not anymore. I stuck to every commitment from that point on.

I enrolled in a technical school and passed a firefighting course. I received college credit for it, but I accidentally missed a written test and was never certified. It turned out I didn't have as much time to study as I thought.

Later I took a truck driving course. I became licensed and drove cross country for a company called Con-Way Truckload. Unfortunately, I was fired after a few mishaps. The bosses said that if I was more experienced they would have kept me on, but since I was a newbie they couldn't take a risk on me.

I have continued to work at low-paying jobs, but since I am no longer a quitter, I have made more money over time. After getting fired by the trucking company, I decided to view developments in my life as steps toward success rather than signs of failure. I may not be thriving in the fields for which I studied, but at least I am getting better at every new endeavor.

Finding a niche in a church has helped me in recent years. Instead of sitting and listening to a preacher talk for an hour, I have become active in ministry. Though I am not a preacher, which is what I was studying to be when I entered college, I feel like I am following in my father's footsteps. He in turn was following Jesus, the perfect example for all to mirror.

I serve as a Sunday school teacher and have discovered the missionary in me, visiting Nicaragua on three occasions. By doing this, I have found my voice. I have accomplished this not by living through another person but by being God's hands and feet.

At the beginning of this decade, an idea came to me. It may have been the craziest dream I have ever had. I decided to write a story that could inspire, entertain, and create a thirst for the written Word of God. The idea created great angst in me. Using mythology to underline areas of the Bible could raise red flags for people. Rewriting the Bible or contradicting it is a serious sin. This is one reason I chose not use the names Adam and Eve in this book. I wanted people to understand that this work is not the Bible but something inspired by it.

So far, my project hasn't created any controversy. I have put the story through strict theological tests by publishers who respect the Bible. I am grateful that these people have stood up for their beliefs, and I hope my story can be a blessing for them.

I find some events in my life difficult to discuss. These circumstances have left a big scar on my heart. This world has cut too deep in many ways. Sometimes I wonder if I will ever heal, but the Bible says sin can be forgiven and reconciliation can happen even in families that have experienced hardships marked by hate.

I am the youngest in my family. My mother, a brother, and a sister are still alive. I have also grown close to three nephews. Satan has plagued us, but he does this to those God calls His own. The book of Job gives us an example of this. People are tested so they may be purified and made stronger for the greater purpose that God has for them.

Maybe someday I can speak about the troubled times, but until a reconciliation takes place certain family members would prefer not to be mentioned. The light is brightest when I write dark passages. Though I may describe moments of great anguish, I know that hope always remains.

I have recently found the Ark of the Covenant in my garage. After cleaning it out, a timeline was found that my dad had made that he used to hang in his church offices. While not literally the Ark, it is something that holds a special place in my heart that helps me feel connected to my dad and God. It is a timeline of the history of the world, including the future. The end of the world is on it through much study by my dad, and the beginning of the new Earth and Heaven are at the end of it. Much thought and detail was crafted onto it, and it represents the hope I look to when I write.

This is the light that shines in the darkness. It is the inspired Word of God as it helps us understand Him and realize that he is with us through the Holy Spirit. He is taking us somewhere in all of this. Dark times will come, but we will have to cling to the right things to make it through it. When we understand this, even joy can be experienced. Not at the end of a timeline that may take centuries before it passes, but today is when the fruits of the spirit can be enjoyed.

There may be a preacher in me, after all. If only I can practice what I preach.

PROLOGUE

The Wisdom Tree

To the south is war. To the west many march to war. To the north is an environmental collapse, starting to spread throughout the rest of the world. To the east is where he comes from; the one who sleeps under the oak tree. Much hardship has led him here to this tree that is rooted deep atop a hill. You wouldn't want to go his way either. The warm breeze will keep any weary traveler from wanting to leave this place.

Here at the Wisdom Tree is a dwelling where no possible harm can ever reach him again. Life lived here comes from a death lived elsewhere, and his price had been paid. Your price has been paid too by a king who had better things to do with his time than to meddle in the affairs of the poor. The poor, however, do not always accept their king.

Patience is needed before we can pass on. To where you wonder? It could be to a home away from home, to dreams fulfilled or to a life without end. It is a place that no man with a caravan of gold can reach. It will require a journey through the eye of the needle. This is a reference to how hard it is for a rich traveler to access the roads into Heaven. It is the equivalent of a camel passing through the eye of the needle. Can a feat be accomplished? It can, but as I said before, patience is needed.

Who am I, you ask? Stories will be he helpful in answering many of these questions. When the man awakens, he will have no memory of his past life. The time he will spend here will be the last things he will remember of a troubled earth. He will never be told exactly what happened to what has been lost, but the stories shared here will help aid him in his reconstruction and preparation for our journey.

What kind of story? In the trunk of the tree a message is carved, saying "In the beginning was the Word, and the Word was with God, and the Word was God. The same was in the beginning with God. All things were made by Him; and without Him was not anything made that was made. In Him was life, and that life was the light of men. And the light shineth in the darkness; and the darkness comprehended it not[1]."

Then came the story, passed down from generation to generation. Man have always been fond of the story. It made the imagination seem bigger than life itself. This made many well-wishers wanting the story to be the Word. Those who would rather not give their hard earned change to the fish understand that the Word is greater than what the story could ever be.

Children acquired a gift. The Word can become hidden in fiction; stories that have the ability to ring true in the end. Stories like the "Pied Piper of Hamelin", "The Boy Who Cried Wolf", "The Emperor's New Clothes", and *The Pilgrim's Progress* are examples of this.

The best kind is the one that causes you to forget your perception of reality, challenges your idea of what you thought was reasoning, and only see the truth in the end. Do you know of a story that has done that for you? Have you heard the one about the hourglass? It is a wild fantasy full of flaws and inaccuracies. The sleeper will be waking soon. Do not forget this moment of our stay here, as it is a reminder of what you've become familiar with. A word of caution to dreamers and to the dreamless: A journey through the eye of the needle has a point of no return.

---

[1] John 1:1-5, King James Version of The Holy Bible

PART I
THE HAMMER

CHAPTER 1

The Invention of Fire

In the beginning, the Word considered the Eye of the Needle in all its worth. What is the Eye? It is believed to be a place between worlds. Many have gone in search of it, only to find a fool's paradise or a vengeful earth, but here it is at the beginning of time.

Now the Eye was of no form and empty of light. Darkness was measured in the shallow of the deep as sand begins to fall. Fear established itself as the link between the Word and the wordless. This fear is the knowledge of deteriorating souls who chose an unfortunate fate. As a keeper of the things to come, an hourglass forms the boundaries of a new age.

Peace and joy reigned in the world long before this fear became known. The hourglass becomes a window into its origin. The sand becomes a snowfall over a desolate landscape. An ancient evil has carried its fear to this place where there is no tree to hide behind. Those who hope for a better world will find it over fire and ice.

A journeyman has already found his footing in this world and begun his progress to find the good proclaimed! Footprints in the snow lead to this wanderer. He searches for someone other than himself who has lost their way. Accompanied with a story, he suffers from a heavy burden. A thick white fur enshrouds his brown-gray hair and poverty-stricken body. He hopes an opportunity to share his story will bury his anguish. His torment finds his voice, as he calls out for a warm body. "Helper, can you hear me?!" From the greenest of greens to the yellow of yellows to the whitest of whites is where he counts his loss.

Past this journeyman, the terrain is pioneered by an elegant and sacred wind. Miles away, a clanging rhythm adds an introduction to a symphony. A mound of snow is the stage. A silver hammer beats it as snow shimmies off at each impact and vibration. An anvil is unearthed as an invisible hand guides the tool, forging its hidden glory. The anvil seems to be a barren table, but there is work to be completed. Mountains are being raised in a far-off place. Stars appear in the vast expanse. A world is being composed. The whistler finds his tune.

"This is my Father's world,
And to my listening ears
All nature sings and round me rings
The music of the spheres"[2]

Beyond this spectacle, a newly furnished cave rests where fallen sand gather, huddling around a dictated flame. They wear only a light robe, and their gloom do not match their white rags. With varying degrees of ruggedness, they look to have gone through extremes. The cold here does not seem to bother them too much. They show a sensitivity to the fire, however.

There is one in the cold heart of the assembly with a perfect, ageless embodiment. He is the only one in the group that isn't bald; an orange afro keeps him at the center of attention. Though he inhabits a young man, he commands much authority in this forbidden conspiracy. They look to him for guidance as they await direction from the one who refers to himself as the New Word. Much history is to be said of this. Much has been sacrificed to bring themselves to this cavern that holds the key to their shared futures.

"What does one wanting to see the truth, call it?" asks the tallest member, standing at the outer rear of the group. His advantageous, lanky stature allows him to gaze over the heads of the rest. An old stick is wrenched in his unsteady hand.

---

[2]   A hymn by Maltbie D. Babcock and Franklin L. Sheppard, 1915

"Fire," shares the New Word. A silent obsession exists within this one that many here believe to be a fearless disposition.

"I've seen it before. I'm not getting near it. What is its nature?" The lofty follower exhibits his cautionary tendencies with nervous twitches. The New Word illustrates his ability to create comfort by instantly appearing behind him. It was a magician's trick no one had an answer for. One moment he stood by the fire in front of everyone's eyes. The next, he was behind all of them, his hand rubbing the nervous follower's shoulder with reassurance. This is his power over them.

"Do not hold back. Embrace it. We have authority over this. It is the beginning of our world."

"Nonsense! How can we make a world?"

"Through invention there can be no end to what this world can be. You must not allow yourselves to speak of the old world anymore. It is of the Old Word. The future must look back at this moment as the beginning of time. The new world will be of the New Word."

The shortest follower holds a large white egg. He squats closest to the fire. He keeps a focusing eye on the ground as the New Word reveals himself back in front of the flame. With a more assured hand, the master holds the stick the tall member had held. With the preserved limb, the false prophet writes in the snow. The word he writes is in the language shared by those gathered.

"What does w-e-r-d[3] mean?" questions the short follower as he stands from his squatting position. He folds his arms as a more stalwart nature exists within this one that most here do not carry with them. There was a time when he considered leaving the flock, but his own ambitious character always kept him close to the New Word. He never wanted to miss moments like this that brought moments of deluded grandeur.

"Our first invention is the fire. Our second invention is called a lie."

"And what does that mean?"

"It's like a story. We make everyone believe I am the Word. That's what it means."

---

[3]   Werd (wârd)

CHAPTER 2

The Mythology

There was no answer from the helper when the journeyman called out to her. A lonely windswept wasteland was what responded. Flights he had been on before, but not in a world like this. He had never been down to this level of seclusion. Aided by the one who loved him or by those who hated him, he had always had someone with him.

It is not an easy memory to keep of his beloved, but it is necessary to remember. He isn't sure what would happen if he were to let go. Maybe the pain would leave him, or it could bring a worse difficulty. This may be the one thing that keeps him pressing on, but it's been too long since their lives were severed by those who tallied their days until they were to die.

Something pulls him outside his thoughts into the world that is his new reality. He looks down at his arms and legs, which are covered, and wonders how he made it so long without succumbing to the elements. The white fur coat he wears is strong enough to keep the snow from soaking into his skin. He found the coat when he woke up in this world. The interior of it was stitched by hands not his own, but by someone with a mastery in tailoring. He is intrigued as to what animal may have been used for the fur. He hopes there were no hard feelings and worries he somehow found the animal who shed its hide.

An unidentified, roaming object is bounding its way across the frozen planet. The journeyman halts in his tracks to brace for what may be heading for him. Its size grows the closer it gets; the shape of a white dog begins to materialize. It soon becomes apparent that this is no ordinary animal. An encounter with a giant becomes a terrifying possibility. Even though it is an animal of unusual size, its head still seems too big for its already exaggerated proportions.

An impulsive reaction from the human propels him to turn around to flee from this unknown threat, but his escape is temporarily halted by an event in the night sky. A giant white bird soars toward him. It is as if it is a gift from the heavens. A transcendent sight, its wingspan is too big for its already impressive features. Its wide reach acts as a glorious crown, even though it is not adorned on its head.

The journeyman chooses his path in the hopes this winged creature can rescue him from a hungry giant. An impressive talent for swiftness is carried with the angelic bird. Its massive wings gracefully beat against the open sky, holding the human transfixed.

Still, a nagging thought causes him to turn his head back toward the lowly dog. The monster's size is still growing, and its mouth is open to show teeth that are possibly the size of a man. He insists on running.

As he hurries toward his choice of capture, the ground underneath trembles, leading toward a distant barking. He senses the hound could pick him up at any moment. Dread mushrooms inside him with every frantic step he takes but dares not look behind anymore. The bird's proximity provides him a faint hope to keep running.

In the possibility the bird could hear or understand him, he shouts, "Help!" Scrambling and yelling simultaneously proves to be too conflicting an effort as he stumbles in his attempt. When he gets back up, the bird seems to have vanished as if it was a mirage. "No!" he cries. "Am I not worthy?" A fear of abandonment brings a different kind of giant—despair. The ground shakes with more violence, causing this hopeless feeling to become unbearable.

The journeyman would have fainted if he hadn't witnessed the end of the rumbling. A brief age came and went. He thinks he was spared somehow. A thick drool glazes over him before full relief sets in. He shuts his eyes, enduring what must have been teeth clamp down around his shoulders. A yanking sensation elevates him off the snow-packed ground. Eerily, the dog hadn't clinched down too hard for smaller bites and an easier swallow.

A draft of wind compels him to open his eyes. What he expected to see was darkness, but what he finds is the whole world. At a thousand feet above the ground, he can view a lot. He can behold endless winter at every point of direction, including the tiny giant far below, who is barking at him from the ground.

He examines what is fitted on his shoulders. Teeth shaped like talons! A flake of a giant feather falls on top of his frost-bitten nose, as he gazes up towards the massive beak. "I thought you were just a dream!" The unique bird doesn't engage in human interaction. "Thank you for honoring me. I may not seem like much, but once I was like you. I'm sure that wordless dog had a taste for delicacy."

He squints to locate where the creature may be fast-tracking him to. "How far does this place reach? I'm sure you've seen it all. Those beautiful gigantic wings of yours must come in handy in a place like this."

The flying man distinguishes a distant clanging echo. He tries to pinpoint the hidden instrument that may be responsible, but his wandering eyes are distracted by endless sights. There is a mysterious structure from the right of the bird's path in the sky. It is something that does not go unnoticed. "Was that an original? It seems like the ground is heading towards the sky over there."

The overwhelmed journeyman finds a spot of courage within him, as he reads the ground to see if the dog is still hunting. There is no sight of it and its teeth. "He'll never find me. I think that thing shall starve now. You can take a break if you like." The bird's altitude remains the same. "I bet you know of a good place to keep a gentle creature, like myself, safe."

He tries his squinting again and directs his tear-filled wonder towards a similar highland, as the one he had questions about. This one is much closer. "Where are you taking me anyway? Is it that big hill over there?" It is a sight that was misunderstood, as it keeps growing in length and width the closer it is. "Wait, that's no hill. I've seen this before in a vision a long time ago. I don't know what it is called."

The mountain he is trying to describe starts to look dangerously obstructive. "Shouldn't you climb a little higher? You're about to fly into it." Instead of scaling higher, its altitude drops toward a concave target on the side of a bluff. Instead of slowing down, the flyer utilizes its speed like a missile. "Are you a mad bird?! This will bring one of those deaths for us, sure enough! I will not be a part of this mischief! Slow down!!!"

He hides his eyes again because he does not want to witness the long-awaited end to his life. When it doesn't pass over, a different kind of air compels him to open his eyes. What he expected to see was darkness, but what he finds is a different world. He could see his reflection cast upon a circular cavern of crystals and precious stones. His withered likeness doesn't belong in a place like this. He wonders why the bird bothered with his kind of trouble. It was a long time since he had similar qualities as the rarities he discovers here.

Another phenomenon captures his imagination. The tunnel is in a constant state of shifting. Even though he thinks he can see the end of this holy place, he can never seem to reach it with his winged escort. The farther he travels, the reflected light shines brighter.

He ponders a mystery, as to how light is being reflected. Where is the source coming from? The intensity of the light becomes too much. No matter how much he wants to investigate the source of this wonder, his eyelids has to shelter to protect his vision.

He swallows a familiar draft. A softening of the light compels him to redeem his eyes once again. He is back outside. The stars that were countless before have become mostly hidden by an ominous black curtain. A foul stench begins curling up his nostrils down to the pit of his throat, releasing a wicked cough. The black veil leads to a new zenith that must have been the highest summit the journeyman has feasted his eyes on yet. A gut feeling says that this is the bird's destination. The closer he is carried to the peak, a shape begins to curl into a nest on top of it. "You're not taking me there, are you?"

A similar presence in the leftward sky is flying towards the nest from a different path. This bird reaches it first. A prize that is gripped in its talons is dropped into it. There is screaming added to the pollution seen here. Even though the journeyman could not locate the birthplace of the light from before, his dread has found its home. A fire is rising from the nest. It burns in a hazy fuel far into the atmosphere.

The journeyman frantically endeavors to shake the bird's talons off of him. He rips into the grip with his teeth as hard as he can, causing the bird to shriek. Deeper into the feet, he buries his teeth, until there is nothing but air to bite into. When the bird released him, he did not calculate if he was already over the fiery pinnacle, or what would happen to him in a free fall a mile above the ground.

CHAPTER 3

Firstborn

I t was a young heaven. The world that was being forged by the Whistler was a place that looked out to the stars, but the stars could not look back. There is a story that begins here. The truth goes back even further.

The firstborn has a dim glow, but it is easy to spot being the only star in a vast and empty universe. Soon the first becomes accompanied by hundreds of stars. What was once a novelty, outshines the newer ones. The original illuminates even greater, casting a shadow over the other stars circling it.

The shadow proves to be a black hole that opened up, swallowing the vehement star. It vanishes, as the fertile night now has one less ornament. The shadow diminishes behind the newborns, as if any trace of the firstborn ever existed.

The hunter gazes at the starry host. A lonely howl cannot hide the hunger that exists within him. A long feathery tail is attached to the end of a body that started giant-sized but grew bigger all the way up to its head. His eyes are covered by ungroomed hair, drooping down, but he can still see through. Nose to the ground, he picks up a scent, causing his massive stomach to grumble. A long tongue hangs down, cracking a steady flow of saliva. His big head arches upwards toward a time long ago.

Instead of heading off on his expedition, he lies down. Patience settles within as he observes his surroundings. Mountains are being raised he could view in a far country. It isn't like the place that he is in where the ground is flat.

The sound of a distant hammer reaches the dog's ears. It is a soft vibrating sensation, but it is enough to create a chain reaction deep underneath the surface. The dog stands to put his ear to the ground. This small tremor underneath sounds like it is rising to the surface.

Topside, a collapse of the ground uncovers a hole in the ice. The frozen floor underneath the mighty dog begins to lower. A steeper angle indulges into a slide, causing the whimpering giant to lose traction. He falls in a spiral towards a bottom that provides no stoppage. There is no perceivable end to it, as the ice continues to collapse around him.

Not too many would believe what happened here. It probably wouldn't make sense for the more reasonable ear, but it is as if the dog descends into the sky instead of the earth. Due to a world covered in snow, it looks as if he is spiraling out of a white cloud.

For the sake of a more coherent story, the corkscrew path straightens, allowing the big head of the dog to shake off its dizziness. One thing is certain at this point, he finds himself at the top of the world. It is much to take in because it is no place for a dog to be on a mountain.

The slide he is on is leading downward and provides no possibility of a subtle descent. A momentum picks up back towards sea level, in a world without any seas. A long tail of drool chases the hound. An illusion of the stars looks like lasers, as a backdrop surrounding him. He easily jumps over a missing piece of the slide helped by the relentless speed. The dog savors the thrilling adventure, with even more drool pouring out of his mouth.

The fun, however, turns on him. An uneven section of the slide knocks him off his easy-going ride, causing him to roll forward. The snowball starts to take effect. Soon the snow that encapsulates the giant grows in epic size.

The ball is almost too big for the chute it is on. It is perfectly centered, without it teetering to the side. An avalanche is in pursuit, which threatens to add more snow to its collection.

When the ball finally reaches the bottom, it continues rolling. The avalanche crashes into the foot of the mountain and poses a hazard no more. A cliff that resembles an ocean wave is nearby, offering a useful obstacle. It is hard enough to fracture the snow off of the grateful captive, as the ball smashes into its wall. The dog is left standing, but the swirling world is too much, causing him to keel over.

When he finds his focus, he stands back on all fours and directs his attention towards a darkness in the far distance. A row of stars in the sky seem to point to a shadow on the ground. It is at the end of a stretch of winter that would prove a day's journey for those who weren't in a hurry.

There is no more hesitation. A giant's hunger burns within him, catapulting his legs into a sprint. Though his legs hadn't been exploited for this kind of pace in a long time, he is quickly remembering his limitations.

The approaching shadow expands into the outline of a human. There is something else. An unidentified flying object is hovering across the open space. The hungry giant can now identify the reason for his instinctive impatience to reach the helpless shadow. This uninvited guest has a similar goal, but it brought with it an advantage. The dog's earthbound legs are no match for an impressive pair of wings. The human doesn't help the matter by running towards the competitor. The dog does have one mercy by having a head start.

When the giant reaches the human, the bird seems to have given up, and the man is petrified. The hunter towers over him and allows his thick drool to glaze downwards. His moment of triumph does not last long.

An attempt at picking him up, by the teeth, is thwarted by a stealth grab by the intruder. He watches the human, dangling like a worm far above the ground and whimpers at his missed opportunity. There is no doubt where he is being taken. The chance he could make it to the summit in time is slim, but the dog is a believer.

The hound races as fast as legs can accommodate, hoping he can discover some hidden ability of flight. This eventually becomes wishful thinking after a couple of leaps into the air that are quite impressive, but ineffective. He tries to roll, but can't unleash the secret of the snowball again.

The bird is too quick. There is no competing, and his belief is greatly tested. He slows his pace and begins walking. His big head hangs, as he wearily releases a moan to the ground, but his faith isn't done with him yet. The dog is not a well-wisher, but he is a dreamer.

There is a faint high-pitched note, piercing the cold air not too far ahead of him. It isn't like the clanging from before, but more like the ringing of a bell. A great wind begins picking up smothering the giant. He becomes lost in it. The giant paw prints he leaves behind is all that can be seen, heading into the blizzard.

Soon his tracks become accompanied by an even bigger set of footprints. They are side by side, as the storm becomes more compact and conical. A moment later the paw prints seem to have ended its walk, but the other set of human-like footprints continue onward.

There would be some who wanted to know who, or what it was that came to the aide of the dog. Certain rules had to be followed. A time would come when man would put up statues or idols to show what they think the other giant looked like. They would never get it right.

The dog and its secret are being held inside the blizzard, as the wind begins to settle. Things become more exposed, but the mystery is yet to unfold. The dog had left his stars and path behind and went to another place, as did whoever was responsible for the footprints.

CHAPTER 4

Cave Painting

The tracks are still fresh. There is a subtle movement in the snow that is not enough to alert a patrolling bird in the immediate overhead. When he is confident that the predator is a fair distance away, a camouflaged lookout stands up. He is clothed in a white-hooded cloak, and he has much to report on his findings. Every step he takes back to his cave he covers up, with the surrounding snow. He must use every precaution to keep a secret to their hideout. It is going to be a long walk back.

The fallen sand have much to fear from these birds of prey. The New Word spoke of a time when there would be sacrifices made, as a result of their choices. They believe the Old Word resents their new found freedom. A long time ago they considered themselves slaves. They were servants to a master that would never share authority.

Once they had names, but they have forgotten them, ever since they were cast out from a place they have no memory of. Only the New Word remembers what it was like. They refused to rename themselves, as an act of independence. The Werd is the only name they care for.

Each of them holds onto an object that is of importance to them but cannot remember why. There are some mixed in with these followers, who do not carry with them these items that are considered paragons-of-past. The scout is one of those whose hands are free.

There is another kind of vagabond, who do not follow either Word. They became lost to a hostile environment, due to a wayward will. These are to be the necessary sacrifices for the new world. Those who remain close to the Werd will be kept safe, as promised by him.

When the scout finally reaches the cave, he is furious. A loud conversation is taking place, immediately outside the entrance. Everything he suffered to do to keep their presence hidden is about to be ruined by these fools. One of them is in a begging gesture on his knees. The other stands, with arms folded in defiance, as the scout approaches them to take charge of the scene.

He unveils his hood, to show his hardened blue eyes, and weathered face that have spent much time in extreme conditions. Though he is someone of a unique fortune, his bald head is a trait he shares with the other fallen. "What are you doing?! Are you two wordless? You'll give away our hideout!"

"We have a deserter who had a change of heart," mocks the defiant guard, who keeps a golden chain wrapped in his arms. "As if he had one." The safeguard has a strong physique and a barreling chest is prominent on him. It is a far contrast to the one that kneels before him. Frail limbs and a hump back is his stature.

"Please," cries the beggar, as he holds out his hands, revealing a leg bone he holds onto. It is his paragon-of-past. "I made a mistake! I see now who the true Word is."

"Now he's out here, trying to give us away."

"Then we can take this feud inside before it is too late!" the scout urges.

"Yes. You're right," replies the guard, as they pull inside a little deeper. When they become convinced they are safely hidden, their conversation picks back up. "The Werd would never allow you to come back now. You have to be made an example of."

"Wait! How did you get here?" the scout questions the deserter.

"I walked. How else would I get here?" The scout rushes back outside and notices a long trail of footprints, leading to the cave.

"Do you ever think about the consequences of your actions? Your tracks will lead them straight here!"

"I'm sorry! I wasn't thinking! I'm wordless out there!"

"Then you will have to be willing to accept a new Word; if he accepts you. You already left him once. I'll tell you what. If you go back out there and cover your tracks, we'll at least present you to the Werd. I can't make any promises as to what his decision will be."

"All of them? They go pretty far."

"I'll tell you when to stop."

**

It feels like hours pass before the deserter ventures past two wall-like cliffs, towering above him. The leg bone he has is long enough to be used as a walking cane. There are still miles of footprints to go, as he wonders how a bird never tracked him yet.

Fatigue catches up with him, as he kneels to regain his energy. He tries to remind himself why he had forsaken the New Word, in the first place. It was an alliance that he didn't hold sacred, considering it wasn't the first time he had rebelled. A long time ago, the Old Word was his first love.

His memory of what it was like, before his initial fall, had faded into a darkness inside his mind. It left him feeling empty, and his current path didn't offer any fulfillment. Maybe things can be different, this time, if the New Word takes him back.

He turns his head back towards the cave, he can still view. The scout waves him back, as he stands to make his return. A thought runs through him. It is possible for one of those white birds to mask itself in the snow. He looks towards his miles of uncovered track and spots a shift in the white landscape.

**

Back at the cave, the scout sits with his back to an icy wall. He ganders towards the snail-like progress, by the deserter, making his return. The guard occupies himself against the wall, on the other side, and has fallen asleep.

A shout wakes him. He immediately pushes himself up, along with the scout. They observe an impatient pace, by the deserter, back to the cave. He is running. "What is that oaf think he's doing?"

"There's something the matter."

From the top of the left cliff wall, rises the white phantasm. It lurks down the wall, towards the desperate runaway, before it swoops down and snatches him up. He continues bellowing, as the bird whisks him away. The two spectators stand in sobered horror, but soon find relief, as the menace left the premises. "Well, at least we won't have to worry about him anymore," reckons the guard.

"Take me to the Werd. I have much to disclose to him." The scout is ushered into the inner sanctum. The fire, the inhabitants no longer huddle around, is still consuming. The fallen sand are scattered throughout a cramped den. Many are standing erect, with heads bowed, facing a pitch black corner. There is something darker, inhabiting it.

"What scandal do you bring with us today?" gossips the Werd. The scout is led straight to this corner, as he faces the dark one, who is peering through a hole. It gives him a glimpse into the outside world. "Where does it hide?"

"Where does 'what' hide?" The Werd doesn't answer, as he steps away from the dark. Him and his hair that has a weird similarity to the fire can be seen more. A grotesque-looking mask is in his hands that resembles a wolf's head. "It has begun."

"I knew this day would be the shadow of our present. You all will be a testimony as to what will happen to those who refused to follow me. They made a selfish choice, unlike all of you, and now they are Werdless. We did give them a chance."

"I found paw prints from a giant dog," the scout reports. "They had quite an impressive scale." The Werd offers a laugh.

"He's probably just hungry."

"There was something else out there. Another set of footprints--" Before he could finish, a sudden wailing from a tunnel fills the hall like a dreaded siren. A member of the fallen sand bolts out of a dark tunnel and seems white with terror. "Why do you interrupt in such a way?"

"I saw something down there!!"

"Is there nothing that does not frighten us? What did you see?"

"I saw a child coming out of a hole in the wall! He was laughing!"

"How could you have seen a child? There has never been a birth. We have seen to that." The scout looks to the Werd, who had retreated back to his corner.

"Go see what it is all about," the Werd commands. The scout follows the fearful follower, dodging the other fallen, who are no longer standing. They are cowering in fear of the news that can only fill them with dread.

They thought the room they are in had only one way out, until now. It is the first time another exit is discovered, as the follower leads the scout to the portal at the bottom of a rocky wall. Crawling looks to be the only way through it.

"Was this the hole he came out of? Where's the offspring?"

"He ran off somewhere. I did see him and hated the very sight of him. The Old Word sent him, I know it."

"Go grab a lit piece of wood from the fire. If we don't know where he went, then we'll see where he came from." The stressed member runs, as he does what he was told. The one thing that has kept them unique from the others that are scattered is the fact that wood was hoarded from the old world. It was something the others did not strategize, but the Werd did. They have enough to last only a little while.

When the follower returns with the fire, the scout can finally see more of the pitiful character. A pink pearl is in his hand and many of his teeth are broken. He assumes the frightened one before him tried to bite into the pearl a couple of times, to help regain his lost memory.

"Follow me," the scout directs, as he grabs hold of the torch and crawls inside the hollow. The other reluctantly lags behind.

The scout can hear the heavy breathing of the one behind him, as they shift through the tunnel. It is enough to cause him to stop, as he turns to face him. "You will need to submit yourself to my authority and do as I say. If there is trouble on the other side, you're state of mind will give us away. Now, calm yourself." The breathing relaxes a bit, as the two continue.

The scout does not have the same fear possessed by the fallen sand, who presumes he is of like-mind. In fact, the mystery of where this tunnel my lead fills him with memories of a time he thought he had forgotten. It makes the future, and what may be ahead for him on the other side, thrill him with reverence. Even though a child led them here, a sense of old is ahead.

The passageway is not as long as they feared. Another room is found on the other side. It is more spacious then the last room they were in. They crawl out, allowing the fire to illuminate a great wall. The scout stands in awe. The follower has the same reaction.

"What is it?" the follower asks.

"He'll want to have it covered up. The New Word will never let this be seen by future generations."

"Who could have made it?"

"I do not know." More memories of his are pouring out like never before, as he finally remembers who it is he truly serves.

"How can we cover it up?"

"Matters like this I would prefer to leave for those who like to stay indoors."

"I know. We'll make our own version." As they crawl out of the room, the fire goes with them. There is still a glow, coming off of the cave painting. It chronicles a story of a giant white dog that would take part in a grand adventure. The glow is a reaction to the fire, as it starts to dim.

There is chatter going on between the two members, filing through the tunnel. "I've got two questions," the follower queries to the scout. "What was that light, and how did that dog get all the way up that mountain?"

"No one may ever know."

CHAPTER 5

Newborn

When the dog opens his eyes, he is no longer snowbound. He discovers himself in complete and unexplained darkness. There is a laid back yelp, as the weary adventurer ponders sleep. There is no way it is happening, considering the fact that the immediacy of getting to the summit in time is still on the front burner. He does not know where he is, in the grand order of things, to even begin figuring out his point of direction.

There is a dim glow, but it is easy to spot, being the only evidence of light in a vast and seemingly empty space. This small newborn star manages to illuminate a fortress of crystals and precious metals. The expanding light shapes itself into a sphere, which shows off an ability to hover.

A shifting in the world draws the dog's attention upward. As if to assist in it's coming, a gaping hole opens up in the rock, ushering in the winged escort. It flies in like a projectile, and the journeyman still hangs like a worm in the bird's talons. Seemingly, the dog is just in time for the expected arrival. The fortress continues shifting, creating a tunnel for the bird to pass through. He feels he is about to lose his chance again.

The dog is still compelled by the splash of light, radiating off of the orb. The light grows fiercer, as the animal walks up to it. By the time he reaches it, the blaze is so great, nothing else can be seen around it, until it winds up inside the mouth of his oversized head.

A shine is casting off of the giant's cavity, as he finds his flair for flight. The orb feels like it is taking control of him. He hovers in the chamber, as he attempts to wield his legs as a paddle to lift himself out of the fortress. The more he sweeps with his legs, the faster he maneuvers.

He bounces off the walls like a balloon filled with helium. It is a hard enough trick to master in a stationery setting, but the cavern he is in does not settle into permanence. The crystal covered walls continue to shift, and the space between them begins to narrow.

The bird had already escaped through a hole that led to the outside world. The possibility of his own escape will have to be accomplished by great velocity and exactness. This proves to be quite a problem. Every time he strokes with his legs, it takes him a little off course, causing him to careen against the wall.

There is a pattern he knew of; locked away in his mind. There is a melody to it also, but he had long forgotten it. He remembers the rhythm, and it is enough to create a balance he needs to straighten his approach towards the egress.

A great speed is achieved in the air that he was never able to reach from the limitations of legs. If only this new level of skill is enough for a contest that is too close to call. The exit hole is shrinking to a point to where a small bird cannot pass through, let alone a giant. It closes up to where light cannot escape.

Darkness is left trapped inside. A treasury of precious metals, making any kingdom the richest in the land, is forever lost. The reflecting light that was once a mystery to the cavern is the one thing that was taken from it. Some hairs that were trimmed off of the dog's tail was added to the collection. The rest of his body is on the other side, where the dog's head is, in a world big enough for it.

Like a shooting firework, the dog carries the light with him and is the brightest aspect of an overcast sky. Heights are reached that he had never dreamed of in the comfort of a soft ground. He starts to lose track of what kind of creature he is. There was a time, he remembers, when he had to look up in order to see a sky that held many delights for him.

There is nothing delightful about this particular night. The mountain he is approaching is a presence that dominates the sky. Stars that were countless before are blanketed by a thick trail of smoke, drifting from the disturbed peak. The dark gaseous output swallows the flying dog, as he ascends and is almost thick enough to smother his light. He has to hold in his breath to keep from coughing, as he looks up for the feathered one he is chasing.

The bird has almost ascended to the top, but the flying dog is picking up momentum in his new habitat in the sky. He reaches the right elevation, when the fowl is already over the pit. The journeyman is falling, with only the fire to catch him. There is only time for one chance to retrieve him.

As the dog scales over the inferno towards the free-falling human, he opens his mouth to catch him. When he collects him, the ball of light falls out. It does not hover any longer, as it drops into the pit.

The dog's talent for flying is brief, as he loses his grip in the sky and plummets towards the other side of the pinnacle. He lands on a path that, in a somewhat perilous way, leads to the bottom. There is no traction on it, but the dog finds the secret to the snowball again.

The backdrop of lasers is accompanied with singing and laughter from a child, who obviously enjoys the visual of a gargantuan snowball, tumbling down a mountain. There is no avalanche this time from a mountain, whose fire burns deeply. Something that was dropped into it from the dog's mouth will have a name to it someday; a newborn seeking a home.

There is not the aid of a cliff this time to fracture the snowball when it finds the bottom, as it continues rolling miles away. It is still padded and intact when it finishes its journey, but the dog is still encased inside. The man is still marinating in the giant's mouth. At the core of the snowball is the absence of light.

After a brief moment of silence, a groaning becomes audible. The groaning increases, followed by a regurgitating sound effect. "Why am I tormented? Where has my suffering taken me?" Sniffing by the human begins to pick up a familiar odor. "Why do I carry the scent of a dog?"

Two giant glowing eyes, displaying a side effect from the orb, opens up through untrimmed hair. It reveals the journeyman inside an icy grave. "Wait, I remember you. You're that villain that was trying to eat me. How did this come to be?" The dog doesn't answer. "You can't talk. You're just an animal." New thoughts begin to form in the man, as to what is really going on here. "You're not that scary. You would have been much more fearsome as a lion. Sooo, you weren't trying to eat--"

As if on cue, the long tongue falls out, picks him up, and returns him back in his mouth. He leaps out of the icy tomb, as he breaks through the top, landing on the surface. The night greets them with clarity, as the stars do not hide anymore behind a dark presence. A frustrated journeyman's body regurgitates back onto solid ground.

"Havoc!" An awkward attempt at standing makes him grumpier. "Would you make up your mind already? Either eat me or let me go!" The giant tongue droops down, as the ever present drool begins oozing out more thickly. It slaps him with the slimy sandpaper surface, knocking him back down. "I see. I'm your plaything."

The giant wanders off, as it surveys the reach of the ball they find themselves on top of. "You were trying to rescue me from that terrible bird. How did you know I needed help?" The journeyman ponders his own answers to the question. "Well, I'll be staying close to you now if that doesn't seem too bothersome."

A great fear stabs at the frail man's heart, bringing him to his knees. "That fire was horrible! They were taking what looked like followers to it!" A different kind of sensation begins to occur in his stomach. "Whew! I'm hungry."

By this time, the surveying dog is on the other side of the ball, formulating an easy way down. The journeyman refuses to face that direction anymore. Thoughts of a fire mountain is something he hopes will become a distant memory. He chooses optimism, as a seed of faith begins to nurture within him. There is unexplored territory ahead of him and wonders what kind of trouble he can get himself into next. This thought of future hazards makes him consider the practicality of remaining on top of a supernatural snowball.

The supernatural part starts to play tricks on him. He swears there is an extra shadow, sitting next to him. After identifying the features of his own shadow, he wonders how he has the ability to cast two. The fact that he is in a new and different world is something he is willing to acknowledge. There is no sun or moon in this place that he knows of. The snow seems to have its own light coming off of it. He begins to relate to what an insect feels like in a domain of giants. There is no foreseeing what kind of surprises he should expect next.

To see if the shadow will follow, he stands up and walks away. A chill crawls down his spine. His eyes refuse to blink, as he stares at the outline that remains a few feet away. The fearful baby steps he takes back towards the eerie shadow does not prevent a slip and fall. Laughing that follows would have angered him if he suspected it originated from something else than the phantom. A child's mirth creates an emotion in him he cannot identify.

He pushes himself up and rubs his unbelieving eyes. The shadow does not reveal itself. "What are you?" The answer comes from a melody from a world he is not ready for yet. Even though he is still terrified, there is something about it that seems like a promise that someone forgot to tell him about.

CHAPTER 6

The Gray Sea

It feels like an eternity is wasting atop the giant snowball. It is enough to inspire sleep for the weary journeyman. As he wakes from a slumber that feels like a grip has taken hold of him, the encompassing stars convey a sense of intimacy. A sensation of being swallowed by endless space humbles him.

As he examines his world around him, he finds the snowball had stretched its boundaries quite impressively. A gray terrain had charted over the ball. It is as if dirt had covered up the ice. An adventurous spirit grows inside of him, as he decides to wander across this mysterious world. He feels he can discover the end after attempting a long walk.

The journey seems easy enough when the strides he takes covers more distance than usual. It feels like he is hopping each step, and the ground is soft for the landing. There are mountains scattered out, but some of them seemed to have burrowed itself into the underground, seeing how there are craters with mountain-sized widths.

He remembers something as he studies his surroundings. The dog has gone astray–or was it him that went astray? "Where did you go?" An echo answers like a distant barking, but there is no other evidence of a guardian.

A light rises from the edge of the world, as he begins roaming towards a beacon that could provide answers. He considers the possibility of a sun in this new age. An excitement fuels a hastening towards this perceived hope.

At the end of his vision, he finds the unexpected. What he presumed was the sun, turns out to be a completely different heavenly body. The white surface that paints it makes it look like the biggest snowball he has ever laid eyes upon yet. "How did I get here, when I should be there?"

The barking originates from this sphere. "Can you hear me?! I seem to be lost again. I never meant to leave you!" He feels lonely being here.

Even though he wants to stay at this particular spot, he finds his legs moving anyway. Something inside of him draws him away from this wondrous vantage point. The feeling of separation grows the farther away he ventures.

The hours fly by crossing an endless gray sea[4]. This place has a certain tranquility about it. The fearsome birds cannot know of this land. It all seems indifferent to him, however. The peace is not infectious and does not care for his suffering.

Another beacon turns on at the end of his vision. Like a moth to a flame, he draws to it. He stares in disbelief at the white ball returning to him. Is he going in circles, or is it a different world? This time he can visualize the dog. The giant is scoping with his big head upwards, as the barking turns to howling. "I'm here! Do you see me?" There is no acknowledgment, and the howling does not cease.

The journeyman's legs has a mind of its own, as it drifts away from this station. The idea he may never find his way back he begins to warm up to. The solitude of this world starts to creep its way into his soul. Maybe he could live here for a spell. He hasn't felt this sense of security for a long and difficult age. Danger is light years away from here.

His investigation extends towards another beacon that turns out to be the white planet again. What he discovers shocks him. The fact that a ghostly face impressed in the white surface would have been enough to frighten, but it is an expression of terror that stares back at him. He wants to flee, but his legs are frozen. A reminder of the horrors of that world convinces him to delay here as long as possible. With closer examination, the phantom face does not seem like a feature of that world, but it has more of a reflective quality.

---

[4]   Sea of Tranquility

His legs begin to migrate again. The peace is even more inviting this time. There is music down this way. The cosmos give a masterful display of brilliant stardust and far away worlds. This is not just a place of inspiration, but it is a sanctuary. The eyes of eternity begin to open within him. His dread finally melts away, leaving behind a memory that is almost too distant to hold on to. It is something he worries he could forget. An overwhelming urge to remain here cannot suffocate the last flicker of memory that shelters within him. Maybe the next beacon can reveal what he cannot not recall.

The haunted face does not beckon him this time. His old mind wanders back to him, as the faded memory becomes clearer. He spies his helper, who is still lost, far away in a world of snow. She is gravitating towards a cliff and appears depressed. "What has become of you?"

He now knows he can't rest here any longer. He shoulders his burden, as the grip begins to loosen. A story is yet to be finished. He comes to one conclusion from his travels on this rock; this universe is big enough for two.

PART II
THE CHAIN

CHAPTER 7

Unchained

In the land of isolation, a woman is gravitating towards the edge of a snowy cliff. There is a bed of jagged, ice-covered, rocks to catch her fall. Unbeknownst to her, miles away, the night sky holds a predator that is zeroing in on its next victim. She is too lost in memory to care and has not known of the dangers this seemingly harmless bird presents.

She plays the part of a beautiful young woman, but with one trait that suggests she may be a lot older than she looks. Amidst her straight amber hair dangles a streak of silver. Here at the edge, her green eyes are all that are exposed, for she is bundled in a white fur coat.

"It's called a horse," a voice instructs that sounds like the journeyman. She is alone on this particular cliff, but her thoughts keep her company, as her memory transports her to another time and place. She finds herself standing in a lush garden. The journeyman is mounted on top of a horse.

Both the man and woman are invisible, except for their eyes that shine through brightly piercing lids. They are like stars that you could only view at night, which is the time of day in this fruitful haven. The dark brown horse, however, is in its full physical glory.

"Horse," replies the woman. "Sounds like something that comes out of your throat." Her eyes float on top of the horse, behind the journeyman, as the sturdy creature takes on two passengers. "Take me somewhere on it, Alphason."

"Where do you want to go to, Evere?"

"I want to see what he could do. Take me somewhere I haven't been before."

As they head off on a cross-country escapade, the horse shows off its tremendous skill. A frolic across the meadow looks like four lightning bugs, zipping across, hovering above the horse. They draw attention from various critters who have to know what it is the horse carries on its back.

Miles are covered in minutes, as the animal's speed is demonstrated. They arrive at a gorge, with a very wide chasm, but the horse hurdles across with ease. The ride is so smooth; they have a sense as if the horse is galloping over wind.

The horse never seems to tire, but sleep is something that can't be resisted for the humans. The ride on top is almost like a cradle for them. They have no clue how long they are out, but every now and again they wake to find themselves in a different area of the garden, with the night still lingering.

There is one moment when Evere awakens she can recount that the horse is flying. It really is galloping over wind. This is a story she tells her husband. He believes her, but it is something he never witnesses for himself.

After an unknown period of time and travel, a shallow stream is forded as water splashes onto them. This reveals their hidden bodies for a brief moment, as the two finally wake to a moonlit drinking hole. They take a break on the other side of the creek, as the horse and its passengers refresh themselves, with the sparkling purified water.

When they situate themselves back on the horse, they divert towards a forest at the end of a series of hills and plains. In the midst of the woods, they find themselves. A great tree rests here, as it shimmers in the night. It has a blue radiance, like no other tree they have ever seen. The woman attempts to unravel a great mystery. They gaze at its low-hanging limbs, while still mounted on the horse. "What is evil?"

"I do not know. The Word commanded us not to partake of its roots."

"Everything the Word has shown me makes me love this place more and more. Whatever it is must be his greatest creation yet."

"Let us not share our thoughts on it anymore. We need to carry on. We were given the responsibility of naming the animal abundance, and we only just begun."

"I love responsibilities. Allow your helper to name the next one."

"Certainly. You can start with this one. He's been following us for miles." The big-headed animal he was referring to is patiently sitting behind the horse, with its long tongue hanging down.

"That, my dear Alphason, is called a dog. I thought you knew?"

"No."

"Well, now you know." Besides its small size, gray coat and eyes that aren't covered by untrimmed hair, there is something about it that seems different than the other animals. It looks ready for an adventure and its heart may be the one thing bigger than its head.

CHAPTER 8

A New Perspective

There is no easy way down from the new landmark, other than a potentially fatal drop that only a giant could survive. The great white dog sits patiently at the bottom of the snowball, licking a paw that throbs from his recent landing. There is a bulge inside his mouth that may explain the absence of a journeyman. The unthinkable happens when he begins to chew.

There is not a cry of agony coming from the interior, but whatever he is digesting starts to make him gag. It is as if his mouth gives birth. Whatever it is, slumping to the ground, has no evidence of human remains. It is hairy and slimy, and has an overpowering stench; something that was ingested from the old world, and the only meal he's had since then.

With heavy reluctance, he plods away, with his big head sagging low to the ground. He peers back at the lifeless journeyman still horizontal on top of the snowball. There is no perceived movement, as he offers a soft whimper.

When he tries a second glance, he stiffens in his walk. The giant snowball and journeyman had disappeared. He runs back and circles the ground that still had an imprint of the ball and the human; stubbing his toe on a small rock. He gives up after he begins to retrace his own paw prints and leaves behind a mystery that has another version to it.

**

The journeyman becomes convinced that he is coming out of a dream and that he is breaking through to the waking world. Though the dream's vividness still has a fresh hold on his mind, a loosening of the grip allows the journeyman to arrive at a familiar level of consciousness. He could remember quite a few details, such as being lost in a strange gray world, where he became separated from his guardian.

He finds himself back on a flat snowy white drift, and the giant snowball he was positioned on top of is misplaced. There is still an imprint he sat in the middle of. The snowball, he concludes, had its effect and will no longer be needed to tell his story. The story that was so burdened with grief had a surprising twist to it, and he is thankful for a new perspective.

A big rock, protruding from the snow, piques his curiosity. He tries to pick it up. The effort is futile, due to the fact it seems part of the ground. He decides to designate this rock as a symbol of his story, turning a new page.

His fur had become wet, after rolling around in his sleep, and starts to become faulty to generate any warmth. The uncontrollable shivering is almost enough to convince him of being awake, but the dog is still vacant. The giant paw prints, surrounding him, debunks any thought of the dog being a dream. A disturbing reminder came to him that if the dog is real, then so are the nightmares in the sky. He examines the atmosphere and finds no immediate cause for concern. He is still drowsy, as sleep becomes a poison. He decides rest can help him forget his hypothermia and hunger.

**

The stars ring like bells, serenading the dog, as he sets out on his next hunt. He wonders what his next step should be, after the man he was appointed to protect seems to have gone astray–or was it him that went astray? The dog becomes unaware of the passage of time since he surrendered the snowball. He follows the stars for his next adventure, as he follows his nose for his next meal.

A danger, mixed with hope, is delivered from the approaching mountainous region. Two white birds uncloak themselves from the snow-tipped peaks, and the dog instantly knows why they are here. The journeyman is still alive, and he is determined to not allow the birds to reach him first. His only lead as to where he is, however, is to follow the two guests.

The birds seem to be returning the way he came from, so the dog turns around and begins a thunderous race in the presumed direction. Thunder, however, isn't quicker than lightning, as the birds pass him over. The believer isn't going to give up this time, but the flyers continue to gain ground.

A strong gust of wind seems strong enough to pick up the dog, but it isn't enough to lift a giant. He is almost back to the hallowed ground that is the last resting place of the journeyman. When he returns, the human is still absent, and a boulder has now replaced the small rock he stubbed his toe on earlier.

He believes he has managed to catch up with the rogue birds. It turns out to be a trick of the senses because the birds aren't flying parallel to the ground anymore. They are ascending into the far beyond of the heaven. The wind carries stronger as if it is chasing the birds, and the dog senses help has arrived.

Above the hallowed ground, the dog sets his eyes to the sky, as the birds escalate too high to view them. The only thing left for him to do is to bark and spectate. He knows that the journeyman is up there somewhere. A great unusual joy unfolds inside of him because he knows he is not alone.

Something righteous does come that disturbs that peace. An inhuman scream chases the wind that follows the birds. The dog turns around and sees what looks like a wave of fire is washing over the region. Flame rains down from an enormous ball that is set ablaze, as it shoots crookedly through the sky. The dog has only seconds to find a safe spot to hide from the flood.

The boulder catches his eye. An instinct leads him towards it because the rock is growing. It becomes big enough to provide a possible shelter from the river, as he scrambles to the other side. The earth growth expands, with a natural arch big enough for him. He crouches underneath, as the river becomes a fiery waterfall, washing off both sides of the archway.

When the last drop of flame falls off, the dog crawls out and notices the fireball transporting up into the heaven, as well. A moment passes, then another moment, as the giant wonders if anything is going to happen. It seems longer than it is, as the dog sits his rear in the snow.

Two falling objects lose its place in the sky. They are smaller balls of fire that crash to the ground. He hurries toward them and finds that the fire has not completely consumed the feathered victims inside. The dog quickly begins shoveling snow on one of them to put out the flame, but allows the other to burn.

The birds are taken care of, but something still aches in him. The journeyman is still being held above him somewhere. The dog directs its attention to the sky once again, as a howl becomes more suitable for a moment like this.

**

An unknown period of minutes or hours pass, as howling wakes up the tired journeyman. He achingly pushes himself erect and the chill has not worn off. The dog seems to be still preoccupying somewhere else. It is dark where he is at, except for a stream of bluish light, originating from an unknown window. It feels like being inside a tomb, or a cave.

He reasons that the light could be a trail to a way out of this place. As he follows the stream of blue, howling leads the rest of the way. It releases an anticipation in him because he knows the guardian to be near. The blue light does not disappoint, as it reveals the exit.

He becomes a witness to an experience he is sure would never be seen again, by anyone. He has the fortune of having a glimpse into an intimacy and remains silent out of respect for the dog, who doesn't seem like he wants to be disturbed.

The governor of the night is back! The dog sings a howl to a moon that has a size that seems fitting in a domain of giants. It almost covers the whole universe, and it seems close enough to touch, as the journeyman reaches out his trembling unworthy fingers. It proves to be an illusion, for the moon is still far away.

Now he knows he is dreaming, as he resigns back in the cave. He prepares for sleep again, as he lays back down. Death seems right around the corner, as the savage hunger starts to become unbearable, and the bitter below zero temperature reaches his bones. He wonders if he will ever wake up again.

CHAPTER 9

Secret Garden

Evere is nearly unaware of the cliff's edge at her feet. The wonder she feels when the white bird gets close enough is a passion she hadn't felt in a long stretch. She can see its big eyes, staring at her from the sky. She feels like she could see another world inside its vision. This moment that is captured helps her forget her despair and remember a time when the Word spoke softly to her.

The Word had a special place for her in the garden. There were things that she could see and experience that was for her eyes only. She found that the horse really did have a gift in flying without wings, but it was through her dreams that stirred it. She would wake to find herself riding horseback in the sky, but she would always be tugged back to her napping.

One night she was able to dream and see where the horse was taking her in the firmament. Small birds were in a formation around her, guiding them to places she had never seen awake. Hours were spent above the ground, and much of it was covered. The garden was a bigger world than she had realized.

It gave her an opportunity to discover new kinds of birds that they were unable to see from the ground. They were birds that Alphason would never see for himself and the names that Evere gave them were one of the secrets that she kept. She would have told Alphason about them, but wasn't sure that they existed outside of her dream.

One thing she was able to gather knowledge of was the fact that there were many creatures in this world, but there were only one man and one woman. It was one of those things that the Word would speak softly to her about. The knowledge that she was being given was the fact that this was a place that not only provided much fruit, but it was important for herself to be fruitful. Time, however, was something that she felt she had plenty of, and there was no reason to rush things.

The horse resigned in following the birds and began adhering to a stream that was growing wider the farther it went. She could not fathom what was at the end of it because the dream began fading.

When she woke, the horse was back, with four legs on the ground, and a small stream at its feet. It was the eyes of Alphason she found, with a new creature he had discovered. The horse decided to take a nap when she dismounted, as she approached her companion. He was bending down, petting a newborn chimpanzee. The mother of the creature was in a nearby tree and was engaged in her own rest. She wanted to tell her husband the places she had seen and the things she had experienced but wasn't ready to share what all of it taught her.

It seemed like the natural thing for Alphason to do, as he placed the young chimp into her arms. The primate looked at her as if she was its mother. It may have been the happiest moment of her life.

CHAPTER 10

The Beast and the Savage

It is the most miserable moment in a savage's life. He thought he would never wake again and he would have been happier if he didn't. There is a warmth to the cave now. It is supplied by a recently sparked fire that burns near a wall. The savage stares at it, with a bleak face. He is reminded of his recent folly. A mountain of perdition is still in his current memory.

A thought also occurs to him that the dog must have found him. None of this fixes his fierce hunger, however. "Where is he? I'm so hungry, I could eat a dog."

The beast returns, crawling through a hole that leads from the outside. What follows is not a cheerful reunion. The savage stares at the beast as if he is dinner. "Listen, you need to do yourself a favor and depart from me. My tendency towards death is making me think strange thoughts."

The savage notices the color red that is dripping from the beast's mouth. "It's nice to see you found something to eat. You didn't save any leftovers by any chance?" The beast exits the cave, as the savage follows him. "Where are you off to?"

Immediately outside the entrance, the savage spots a trail of life force, leading to a carcass of feathers. "You killed one of them?" The enormous showy moon had shrunk to its normal full moon size. The savage has a nice view of a land littered with flame. "What happened here?"

There is something else in the forms of human footprints in the snow that makes the size of the paw prints seem reasonable in comparison. "Who else was out here?" The beast ignores the questions, as he leads him to the carcass and begins rationing a section off. The savage follows suit, as he grabs a handful of raw meat and introduces it to his mouth. He immediately spits it back out. "Uhhh! How can you eat this? It's disgusting!"

The beast portions another section off of the carcass, as he carries it inside the cave. The savage shadows him and observes him dropping it in front of the fire. "You want me to offer it to that? Would it make it taste better?"

The savage is about to ask him what the fire is already consuming, but his question is answered by white feathers scattered around the area. Inside the fire looks like a beak has not completely burned up.

He lifts the fresh bird meal they just brought in with them and heaves it into the heart of the flame to join his companion. The beast whimpers, as he hurries back outside. The savage drags the charred remains out and tries a taste before he spits it back out again. "This is going to take some time getting used to."

The beast caters to another section, bringing it inside, placing it in front of the fire again. A wooden stick happens to fall out of his mouth, as well. "How's a stick going to make it taste better?" The beast pokes at the flesh with its claw. "You want me to insert the stick into it?" The savage obliges, as he raises it up with the small tree limb. "Now what?" The beast stares intensely at the red and orange, as the savage spears it into the center of the flame. Barking from the beast prompts him to pull it back out. The meat is still in favorable condition, as he holds it close. "I see, just keep it near. I'm sure that will help."

The educated journeyman comes up with an idea, as he begins to twirl it. "I bet this will make it taste good all the way through." He begins blowing through pursed lips and finds that whistling is something to be mastered. A cry of loneliness comes from the dog when he hears this. "What's the matter with you?" He looks back at the end of the stick and sees no immediate change yet to the raw meat. "This might take a while."

Suddenly, something completely out of place hits him. "Wait a millennium! Where did you get this stick?! I haven't seen a tree since I left home!" He drops the stick and meat into the fire again and clumsily rushes outside. A small bare tree had sprouted next to what is left of the bird. "Where did that come from? It wasn't out here before!"

CHAPTER 11

Noel

The fallen sand left their cramped den and situated themselves in a new hall. It is the one that was found by the scout and the frightened follower. There is still a mystery to it, for much of it is still unexplored. No one seems too interested in going deeper than they already are for fear of stumbling onto the child again. There were others who claimed to have seen him again, or heard his singing. It is enough to keep everyone on edge.

The fire was also relocated from the old room, placed in what was presumed the center, but the wood they had had officially run out. The fire is weakening, as everyone's false sense of hope diminishes. Some of them are considering going back outside and taking their chances with the birds. The Werd has a lot of work to do. It is up to him to bring comfort and convince them that his way is still the better way.

He stands in front of the dying fire and seems to be postured for a speech. In his hand a pink pearl is held. It looks like the one that the frightened follower carried. "You all tremble as if the moment this fire dies so will our futures. I have brought you all this far. Let not this fire blind us. There is so much more to see. I want those closest to me to grab a handful of dirt, snow or whatever you find and throw it into the fire." No one seems to have the nerve to move. "You are wondering what would happen if you were to do this. Trust me. It is something that needs to be done. Go ahead, do as I said."

One finally moves. The others follow his example, grabbing what they can find, tossing it into the fire. They had no knowledge that this would smother the flame, but all of them now stand in complete darkness. "What is this?" shouts someone in the black. "You tricked us! We can't see anything!"

"Of course you can't," the Werd responds. "This was going to happen eventually. It is better to not be a victim of circumstance, but be in control of your fate. We did not need this fire, for I will now tell you about a prophecy that will be fulfilled at our coming present. I will need volunteers here soon to take on a very important mission. This land, you see, will start growing. There will be trees everywhere as far as the eye can see. Those volunteers will be the ones to gather the harvest, and bring them here to build a new fire. It will be one that will never die."

"How could we possibly accomplish this? Those birds will hunt us, and we will never be able to find our way out of here for lack of vision."

"You have no vision on your own unless I provide you with one. I will take care of those dreadful birds. Their day will come to an end. This security will not be provided for you unless you do what I say."

"So we just sit in darkness until this prophecy comes true. How long will this be?"

"It may be already happening. Who will be my first volunteers to find out? It will have to be those that love me the most."

"I will go." It is the scout who speaks.

"I knew I could never doubt you. You will need a couple of others just in case you find something. You will need to bring back some wood."

"I will select them myself."

**

"So how is it that you know a way out of here without being able to see?" Asks one of the two selected, as they follow the pathfinder through the darkness. Their guide exudes fearlessness in a time of doubt.

"What? You never anticipated this day would happen? Did you really think that wood would last? It is my job to chart whatever territory I am in whatever the circumstance. Don't worry. We are near the exit. You should be seeing light soon."

Light emerges around a rocky corner, as relief is heard among the small party. "I think we should probably get to know you a little bit better. We can become quite useful to you."

As the scout looks them over, he notices that one of the followers is taller than the other, but they are of similar weight. Extra long finger nails dangle at their sides. It is something that the scout has in common. Most of the fallen sand have chewed their finger nails down to stubs, but the two that stand before him are different. Both of their hands are free of paragons-of-past.

They have another distinction between them. The shorter one has a baby face, while the other looks like his old age is clearly showing.

"I was hoping you would say that," the scout replies. "We have much to discuss as we look for the wood."

They stop, just short of exiting, as they stare at the exposed ground ahead of them. There is no bird in sight yet, but they wait for the scout to make the first move. "If you want to survive, you must do as I say. There will be no talking unless I speak first. You can expect at least three birds, maybe four, on our search. That is the usual number I see while I'm out. I have been spotted a couple of times, but knew exactly what to do when it happened. It will be slow moving from here. You two can take turns, but the one who takes the rear must cover up our tracks with the snow. Understood?"

"I see no tree from where I stand," the shorter one points out. "How do we know which way to survey?"

"I will head towards a region I have not explored before. If the first tree had sprouted, it would most likely come from there. Let's go.

**

A day passes since they left the cave. Three birds had been spotted since, and the party's presence has been kept secret. The whole time the scout had never spoken, so the other two stayed quiet, as well.

The taller one starts to get impatient, as there is something he just couldn't hold back anymore. "What was it you wanted to discuss with us? We've been out here an entire day, and you haven't said one word."

"Quiet," the scout whispers. "I rarely see three birds in one day, which means they are hunting this territory. This is one reason I have not gone this way before. I believe this is the direction towards the mountain, but I have never been there myself. Their hearing is just as powerful as their vision. Do not lose patience. We will need to be out here for at least two more days. If tomorrow comes and only one bird is seen, we will speak again. Not until then."

**

Not one bird is seen the next day. The three decide to take a break in a low spot, surrounded by rolling hills of snow. "We can talk, but do not get too comfortable. We are still exposed. Anything can happen."

"Will you share with us your words now?" the baby-face asks. "Lead the discussion as you see fit."

"I have a name. There is no forgetting it."

"Can you still depend on the Old Word after what you've done? Why do you still hold on to it?"

"My name is Noel. You will probably turn me into the New Word after what I tell you. I will now reveal my other secret. There is no rebellion in me against the Old Word."

"This is rabblerousing," declares the tall one, pointing one of his long fingernails toward him. "We will turn you in to be certain."

"It will be an exceptional fluke, finding your way back. You will need me."

"Right you are," admits the baby-face. A peculiar nature exists in this one, as he begins building snow at his feet. They almost look like animals, but the shapes he is forming are unknown, even to himself. "Someday, I would like to know what these mean." A small glimmer of hope can be seen in him, as he looks up to Noel. "The tall one does not speak for me."

"I am not one of the fallen," Noel continues, "but sometimes things get mixed in with the sand. Sometimes you find treasures buried underneath it, but the sand, to be sure, is dead. I am alive."

"Why are you so persistent on coming out here so much?"

"I'm trying to find the one who set me free. It was a long time ago, but ever since it happened, I became more reminded of my history. The Old Word chose me, along with others, to lose our memory, experience the fall from infant eyes, and to be restored by the man the Word created. I choose to stay hidden among the sand, in order to find those who have also been appointed, and venture out here at every opportunity to search for Alphason. I know he still lives. I compel you to not share with the New Word this feeling I have of the possibility of his survival. The New Word will want his life force shed."

"How do we know if we are one of the selected? Won't we need the presence of Alphason to be restored?"

"As I've said, my memory has come back to me. I know exactly who else is there. Have you two ever wondered why your hands are empty, unlike the others? Both of you have been chosen. I will need to bring you to Alphason, or bring him to you, for your lives to be as mine. Do not trust the so-called New Word. A fool is leading the blind."

"Do you know our names?" asks the taller one, masking his emotions, with a stubborn skepticism, and a leathery face.

"I do not. It is one of the few things I have no recollection of."

"You are a liar! The Werd is the only name that matters."

"Because we were given infant eyes to experience the fall, there are some of us who have grown accustomed to the New Word. I ask of you, however, do not expose me yet, till you have further knowledge of the truth. At least allow me a chance to find Alphason first."

"We'll give you that chance," agrees the baby-face. "Won't we?" This was directed to his taller peer. "Noel is our protector out here. We owe him that much."

"Fine," mumbles the taller one. "Answer me one last question. If you are with the Old Word, how come you are frightened of the birds?"

"We are not the only ones who have a lot to learn," answers Noel. "Their minds have become infants, as well. They have not figured out who I am yet to discern the difference. Much of the Old Word's creation has gone under this. The birds seem to be learning, however. This is probably how I've survived for so long. Let's continue our journey. There is one other area to be searched before we should head back."

**

Their return to the cave is empty-handed, but the three are relieved to make it safely. They pause before entering, as fear is heard, coming from the darkness. Crying and moaning is what carries to them from the depths. "I don't think I want to go back down there," proclaims the tall one. "I think I'll take my chances with the birds."

"You're starting to think like me," responds Noel. "The two of you stay here. There are a few more down there who need to be rescued, as I share the news of what we did *not* find to the New Word. He must not know of our identities, for they outnumber us."

As the scout enters the cave, the two that stay behind hears singing coming from the interior that sounds like Noel. Soon a second voice begins to harmonize with him. It is higher pitched, like a eunuch. The child had found a friend.

CHAPTER 12

Curiosity

The distracted quarry puts up no fight or flight as she stands poised on the very edge of the frosty precipice. She continues gazing into the eyes of the misunderstood bird she considers befriending. It is too easy of a steal for the invader, as it yields its descent to set up for its capture.

Before the flyer could lay one claw or feather on her, a tall leafless tree shoots up from the bottom entangling it in its web of branches. When it releases itself from the trap, it becomes a victim of gravity, as it plunges helplessly to a bed of jagged rocks.

Painful bird noises interrupts the woman from her heavy ponderings, as she becomes more aware of the downed flyer. Instead of fear, she feels compassion for it. She locates a path, leading to the bottom of the drop-off, as she makes her way down. The hapless bird had violently cascaded off the rocks, into a softer bed of snow, next to the newly crafted tree.

The helper reverently approaches it and naïvely begins to examine its massive wings. They are too great for her, and the flightless bird squawks from irritation when she tries to lift them. "Why would you fly into a tree?"

She begins to sob, as a haunted memory returns to her. "This is all my fault why this happened. There was a time when accidents like this never took place. If Alphason were here, he'd know what to do. He took care of the animals, while I tended the garden."

Her melancholy begins to overshadow her as it makes her feel she is still there. "If it makes you feel any better, I don't much care for trees, either. I hope you like stories."

Midnight in the garden held a secret, as the horse, and its duo had found a nesting spot on a flat grassland. It was at the perimeter of the forest. A signature of two invisible bodies seemed to by lying on bended blades of grass, which gave a wave-like effect. Someone was turning over.

A distant barking woke up a sleeper. It was Evere. Her eyes flickered on close to the ground, as they levitated, and the grass underneath lurched up.

The disruptive barking seemed to have ceased, momentarily. A heartwarming sight greeted her eyes. Trimming the tallest tree, a massive pale beast, with a long thick neck, and even bigger legs was having its late night snack.

She strolled over to it, and the behemoth sensed no cause for alarm. [5]He ate grass like an ox. His strength was in his loins, and his force was in the navel of his belly. He moved his tail like a cedar: the sinews of his stones are wrapped together. His bones were as strong pieces of brass; his bones were like bars of iron. He was the chief of the ways of the Word.

It allowed her to bear hug its tree trunk legs. The tighter she would squeeze, the greater her joy blossomed. There was nowhere else she would rather be.

She should never have let go, but something stole her away that night. There was something foreign inside of her she did not have a word for. It was staring back at her when she looked at it.

The ground she trusted upon had a slight incline that descended into a lake at the bottom. She spied an oddity in the lake showcasing a large reptile-like head above the water. It was a shy creature, but it seemed very interested in Evere. Its seductive eyes would not detach itself from her. She considered going down and introducing herself to it but noticed

---

[5]   Job 40:15-19a, KJV

the water he hid himself in was at a boil. There was an absence of fear in her, but an existence of something else.

The distant barking began again, and it was coming from somewhere deep in the forest. Evere tucked away inside as she followed the trail of sound, coming from the hidden dog. It was the gray one that followed them on their tour of the garden. The dog stood in a small break in the trees that allowed the moon to peer through. He was viciously growling at a strange shadow that the light would not illuminate yet. She had no understanding of the protective nature that existed within the hound. "What is it? There's nothing there."

She was wrong. Another pair of eyes were staring at her, but much smaller. "Two new creatures in one night it seems. I must go wake Alphason. He needs to see them first. They should have names."

"On the eve of revelation, there will be no need for such a trifle." The shadow was speaking. It was a kind, male voice that carried its words with skill.

"What are you?" The creature entered the moonlight to reveal its hidden form. It had four legs, a long back, a forked tongue slid in and out, and looked unlike any lizard they had already discovered.

"You were told to name the animals, but as you well know, an animal cannot speak."

"The Word must have sent you." The unusual serpent seemed to writhe at her statement.

"I did come to see you."

"What was that other creature in the lake?"

"Him? Wouldn't you like to be the first to behold its wonder? He is a shy one and will only come out at the right moment, but there is something holding him back."

"He is a mighty creature from what I anticipate. What could possibly hold him back?"

"A chain that you cannot see keeps him imprisoned."

"All of this is too confusing. I do not know of a chain and what does 'imprisoned' mean?"

"These questions can be answered if you allow me to show you something. Come with me deeper into the forest." She followed its long tail, as it led her back to the tree that Alphason and her visited earlier. The tree still had a glow to it.

"Is this what you wanted to show me? I've seen this tree before."

"You have never truly seen it. There is a side to it that you cannot see unless you fulfill its purpose."

"It has a purpose?"

"Yes, and it involves you. In order to see more of what this tree has to offer, you will need a little more of what you already have."

"And what is that?"

"It is known as curiosity. You already have some of it. This is why the tree graciously gives off its light. It wants to share more."

"If curiosity is what is needed, how do I acquire more?" The serpent scurried toward her and clamored on top of her invisible shoulder.

"I want you to close your eyes." She did. "I want you to imagine everything that the Word has made and shown you, up until now."

"I am, and it is magnificent. There is so much to love. I am humbled at being included in all of his blessings."

"Now," the serpent seemed to be whispering this next part, "I like you to try and imagine everything that you don't know about the Word and hasn't revealed to you yet."

"That's impossible. How can I imagine something I haven't seen before?"

"By opening your eyes." The tree revealed its secret. The light seemed to go hazy when she opened her eyes. The shine became so bright it was as if daytime had suddenly arisen.

"What did you do to it? The light is blinding me."

"It's not what I did to it. You will need to give it a moment. Your eyes will get used to it soon. Just try and focus." Clarity started to sharpen the fuzzy edges, but when things became clearer she became awestruck at what she beheld. At each low-hanging branch of the tree, an image were like fruit. They were like windows into another world. Evere approached it closer and fell on her knees. It was the only response she could manage for what she saw.

"What am I seeing?"

"It is everything that you do not know of the Word yet. The knowledge of good are the treasures found in the past, present and future."

"What about evil? Does it not show that?"

"For that trick you will need its sustenance in order to have its provision."

"I can't. The Word told us not to eat of it, or we shall die." The serpent climbed off her shoulders and stood in front of her. The light blinded her again, but she could almost make out what looked like an outline of a human.

"You will not surely die. For the Word knows that if you eat of it you will become like one of us, knowing good and evil. I cannot show you my true image without first you taking your share of the tree. There is another side to you as well. You are a very beautiful woman. The Word sees it, as do I. The Word has kept you from knowing your true self."

"This must be why Alphason is hidden too."

"It is. Your curiosity has already given you new eyes to allow you to see the chain that imprisons us all, but you are still unable to understand what it is for. The tree can release us all."

"Good can come from this." The man returned to his serpent-like form, as she held him in her hand. "Good *and* evil can come from this."

"There is one other thing. The Word already knows that you are going to take of this tree. It is predestined that one day it will happen. Why avoid it?"

"What a revelation."

"You are not ready. There is no hurry. Visit here every night to see what the tree has to offer. Someday you will see something in it you cannot do without, and you will eat its tasty fruit. The fruit really is quite delicious."

As Evere made her return through the forest, a chain, with an unearthly green glow lying on the ground, gave her an optional path out. The talkative serpent made her wonder about all the things she could learn. She speculated where this chain would take her, but decided to follow the gray dog instead. It had some of its own secrets Evere wanted to know about. This nonverbal creature would faithfully lead her back to Alphason. It was enough curiosity for one night.

CHAPTER 13

Where it Leads

The gray dog was once unencumbered from a protective nature. Its only purpose was to grab hold of every new and unusual smell that bloomed across the garden, like a flower on the first day of spring. He almost had the land mapped out and categorized, based on what scent seemed native to a specific region. It was daytime in the garden, but to him everything looked black and white.

His master was a very busy sort that would greet him once a season, and it has been a long one since he was able to be at his side. So many new fragrances he wanted to share with him about. The day was finally here. The whistling was the first thing he heard.

The Whistler had a likeness that only the dog knew of, and it was to be kept secret. The hand of the forger pointed at a path that led over a hill, as the master had a new task for him. Something new was constructed inside the animal. The dog was now a protector for the ones to be walking over the horizon one day.

Many days later, on the evening of the encounter, was followed by many sleepless nights for the big-headed hound. The two humans were sleeping at the outer rim of the forest that held the curious tree. The dog kept watch over them and found few opportunities to rest.

A serpent-like creature, with four legs and a long tail, was slowly approaching one of the invisible bodies. The dog immediately rose and dashed towards the startled serpent. They both ran into a forest that offered many places for a small creature to hide.

A small, moonlit break in the trees was reached as the warm-blooded creature decided to quit running and play dead. The dog was not fooled by the lifeless body of the legged serpent on the ground. He began to growl and bark at the deception. Soon the woman entered the break and found the invader, but she showed no signs of fear of it. The seducer led her away towards the tree, as the gray dog followed them.

He should have stayed with them, but the dog became distracted by a green-glowing chain, lying on the ground. His old instinct of exploring his nose had come back. The dog was compelled to follow the link to see where it would take him. An adventure could not be ignored.

The chain was very easy to follow, up until the point it separated into two chains. The dog wondered which way he should go. Looking up towards the stars usually gave him an answer. Even though the dog could only see black and white, the stars were the only things that showed color to him. He saw as many various colors as there were stars to be counted. This particular night, however, gave him no answers, so he had to choose his own way.

He decided to follow the left chain, or it could have been the right. The dog did not know which the difference was between the two, for the chain he followed would only lead him to a third chain that led a different direction.

After more forks in the road, he began to lose track of where he was going. This was unusual for a dog who knew every smell to this place. A prison began to form around his mind the more he would follow a new section of the chain. He wondered if he will be able to track his way back to Evere, who he was supposed to protect.

The dog halted in his tracks and hung his big head low to the ground. It was the first time he ever whimpered. He needed courage to find his way again, as he began to howl.

Something caught his attention at the surrounding trees. Small bells hung high on some of the trunks that played gently against a patient breeze. It seemed like a different path that was not his way, but somebody else's. He decided to leave his dependence on the chain and investigate where the bells might lead him.

They seemed to be going a random direction, but his heart began to warm the more he would follow them. He felt a presence in the forest with him. There was no fear from the dog, but a sense of kinship was found in him.

Goliath feet were discovered. He didn't see it at first until he obliviously ran into a bare toe that was the size of him. They looked to be human, but the legs extended through the top of the crowded trees. There was no seeing pass the limbs. The dog wasn't sure what questions were answered from this sighting, but the path he was on promised more of an explanation.

More bells were picked up again and the trail led him at one point outside the forest for a brief moment. This provided a window to a different perspective on the green chain he was no longer following. It was like a spider-web. Thousands of intersections, all leading up to the sky that was being held by some unknown source. It was as if there was a giant up in the heaven somewhere; weaving its pattern and keeping it secure.

The dog now understood the chain and what it was for. He understood why he was chosen to watch the humans. If ever a day would come that this chain was broken, the humans would need much more than a gray beast to protect them. They will need the Word himself.

The bells proved to be helpful, as they led him back towards Evere. She seemed preoccupied with the chain herself. The dog hoped a bark would lead her away from it, and thankfully it did, as he led her back towards the sleeping Alphason.

When she finally laid back down, the dog placed himself between the woman and the forest. It seemed there were many things to protect his people from. It was going to be another long evening, as he continued to stay awake to keep watch over the humans he was appointed to protect.

CHAPTER 14

Something Luminous

After Alphason had finished his bird meal, he emerges from the cave after a long period for the first time and seems to be energized. "I haven't felt this strong for a long time! I feel like I can take on anything, including those birds." He begins shouting to the sky. "You hear that you annoying, condescending things up there!? You think you're better than me? I'm not afraid of you anymore!"

The giant white dog crawls out of the small opening of the cave, stands by the man's side, and looks to the atmosphere for any sign of activity. His man tilts his head up to the giant. "I may not need you anymore. I appreciate everything you have done for me, but I think I can manage those winged fools myself. You were a good companion. This is where we must leave each other. You see, I cannot stay here any longer. I need to find my helper. We've been idle for too long. Thanks again, but goodbye."

He heads off in a random direction, as the dog obediently stays put. A minute later Alphason wanders back. "You think she may have gone this way instead?"

He starts walking in the opposite direction, as the dog watches his progress again from where he sits. It takes him an extra minute longer, but the man faithfully returns. "I guess I should practice a little more humility. Once I ate the strength of the bird, I thought anything was possible. You will have to accompany me further. I just need help finding Evere, but the birds I can take care of."

Before they head off on their newly revived journey, they stand for a moment on the edge of a vast world, covered with a seemingly never-ending winter. The man waits for the dog to take the first step. "So which way do you think she went?"

Instead of looking forward, the dog searches the stars to find his answer. "She couldn't possibly be up there could she?" One particular star begins to shine brighter, and the dog was already moving in the direction of it. The man runs to catch up. "So we're off then, aren't we? You seem to know where you are going."

Hours had been passed on the journey when the man decides to ask some questions that are taking up most of his thoughts. "Do you have a name?" The dog stays silent. "Of course, if you did have a name, there would never be a way you could tell me. If it is okay, I would like to give you one. I'll need to call you something. There was a time when I was supposed to name all of the animals. Evere, herself, was the one to first call you a dog. You, however, shall have a special name. A name for a dog above all dogs, for there is none I have ever encountered like you. Let's see. What shall it be?"

The man thinks about it for a few paces until one pops into his head. "How about Snowball?" The dog peers down at him strangely. "You don't like it, do you? I'll find a different one. Well look at you, you're big and can disappear in the snow like a snowball, or a ghost. A ghost is what Evere and me would call something that could blend in with its environment. That's it! From this day forward, you shall be called Ghost." The dog shows no sign of disapproval. "No grumbling? Good. We are both satisfied."

The man has other thoughts itching at him, as he looks up to the heaven. "How come there is no sun in this place? Back in the garden, we had what was known as day time. When the sun had rose, it would feel you with this indescribable warmth and would make you feel as if you were the brightest jewel the Word ever created. You should have been there." Ghost looks down on him with another strange stare. "And there was this tree that was taller than any tree that was ever made. It was even bigger than you."

His reminiscing begins to make him feel as if he was still in the garden. The moon looks to be replaced by a sun that shone down on a beautiful landscape, untouched by winter. There was a shallow spring that a deer was drinking out of, along with a lion who seemed to not notice the other. A path of flowers, near the stream, led over a hill.

Something luminous was coming over that hill. It was Evere and Alphason, who were taking a stroll. They were still mostly invisible, but a shine was now coming off of them. It outlined their hidden forms, like a jewel giving off its light when the sun beamed down on it.

They stopped at the spring to give the two animals, who were still drinking its goodness, some attention. Alphason noticed that Evere was not looking at the animals but had her focus at the direction of the forest. "You seem to be preoccupied with that tree, lately. You've been going in there every night. Have you forgotten about the Tree of Life? We were given permission by the Word to visit it anytime, and eat its life-giving fruit. This stream will lead us right to it. It is a three day journey from here, but I have never been there myself. Can you accompany me on this walk?" Evere seemed interested, as his news finally distracted her thoughts.

"Sounds like a grand adventure. We should go there right now." As the two followed the stream, something else was coming over the hill they were just on. The gray dog was keeping his distance, but still followed, keeping true to the master's calling.

**

"It wasn't enough, however, to keep her from going to that other tree," shares a sad Alphason, on his journey with Ghost. "We didn't really know what it was called then, but we now know it was The Tree of the Knowledge of Good and Evil that caused us to stumble. She blames herself, but it wasn't her fault. I was just as interested in that tree as she was, but I never showed it." Alphason appears troubled by his story. "This is too depressing of a memory for such a heavy journey. How about a lighter topic to lighten the load."

He looks up at the stars again. "You know, this sky does have its moments. You are going to think I'm crazy, but I get a strange feeling, sometimes, that there is a door up there somewhere. I am going to reach it, and it will take me away from this place, someday."

As the journeyman and the mighty dog continue their trek, above them in the heaven, the moon no longer hides. The stars give them hope. A wooden door, oblivious to the travelers, with a shape of a wise old tree carved in the upper center, hangs in the sky, at the edge of their imagination.

PART III
THE SWORD

CHAPTER 15

The End of the River

A stream that grew a half mile wide and became too deep to walk through could no longer be considered a stream anymore. The river that Evere and Alphason had followed was one of four that led to their desired destination. Each of them dispersed to different areas of the garden, providing it with life. It was supplied by a tree that was easily the biggest landmark in the garden, with the Word as its planter.

Evere and Alphason stood in awe at the edge of a giant pool. It was poured by a waterfall, coming from the trunk of the great tree. The tree was the closest thing to a mountain in their known world. Its massive branches loomed over their heads, offering a shade. Thousands of fruit, with as many different varieties hung, but were too high to get to.

The invisible humans entered the pool. Swimming seemed the best way to experience their day. There was no weakness in them, as they were able to swim to the very center.

As they kept themselves afloat, Alphason scanned the land around them. There were various animals, grazing the banks. Some were staring at the ripples in the pool, caused by the wading, invisible humans. Evere had her sights on the high branches above, where there was something that was presenting quite a conundrum for them. "How are we to get to the fruit?"

"Maybe we could try climbing the tree?" suggested Alphason, as he looked up to where she was studying.

"I'm not sure that would be the best way."

"There's a way. The Word will provide it. In the meantime, we should explore what we can." Alphason had to know how deep the pool was, as he attempted to dive the full depth. It felt like a mile to get there, but the bottom was discovered and a soft bed to place his feet. There was no need for breath down here.

When he looked around him, he saw a very unobtrusive, open world. His eyes gave off its inner glow again, as he was in a place the sun could not reach. There looked like four legs dog paddling at the surface that he could see above him. He had a good idea what gray furry creature they belonged to.

Down where he was, a killer whale was spotted navigating the bottom. He swam towards the creature and found a hole in the floor. The hole was big enough for him and the whale to swim through, as he poked his head through it. It felt like he came up for air, but he certainly wasn't at the surface. It was a chamber like no other. He had somehow found himself in the heaven he could only view from the footstool of earth. The place seemed to go on forever. It looked like a home for the stars he sees at night.

The hole opened into what seemed like a current in the middle of space, as various kinds of whales were passing by. From the dwarf sperm whale to the great blue whale, was the visual majesty on parade. Where they were going was left up to the imagination. Endless amounts of exploration were provided, by this tree it seemed. He decided not to venture any further and return to Evere; leaving the possibilities of where this hole could lead for another day.

As his head reached the surface, an apple landed on his head. It caused Evere to laugh. "You've been down there for quite a while."

"We definitely need to come here more often. I believe this place offers a way to visit the Word's home if we wanted to." Another piece of fruit landed in front of them, as they look up to notice more of it falling from the branches. Evere grabbed a peach and ate it.

"I've never tasted this kind." All of the fruit that were falling into the pool began to float towards land. As the first piece of fruit reached the shore, it miraculously changed its shape. It morphed into a tan rabbit that hopped away towards a more fitting habitat in the garden.

"Did you see that?" When the next piece of fruit reached the shore, it changed into a Sumatran elephant. This creature stomped away in a different direction than the rabbit.

"I've seen this before?" Alphason seemed surprised, but not angry at her reveal.

"You led me to understand that you have never been here."

"I haven't."

"How could you possibly have accomplished such a trick?"

"I saw it in a vision in the other tree."

"All I saw in the other tree was what looked like any other tree, except its unique ability to give off its radiance, like you and me."

"You have to know how to see it. A creature had told me how."

"How could an animal have told you? I thought they were unable to speak."

"This one could. It looked like a lizard, but unlike any we have seen before. I'm going to go back, and you should come with me. This was a journey worth taking. I would go anywhere with you, but I would dearly wish for you to accompany me back to the other tree."

"No, thanks. I think this tree will offer more than enough pleasure to enjoy to last an eternity."

CHAPTER 16

A Tale of a King and His Many Wonders

There once was a king that sat upon a throne. He was rich with many wonders, as he waited with endless patience to share his vast abundance. There were many stories to be shared, and an eternity was his stage. He was in no need of an audience, but those that wanted to listen allowed his joy to magnify. His creation was an expression of his love.

There were those who had no interest in his tale and chose to be cut off from his roots. Some who were severed were truly regretful and longed for a day to hear the king's words again.

Eternity was about to have its moment in history that will carry out his wonder across many generations. The fruit will fall at first, but only to spread his seed to grow new trees. Let not the poor be troubled, but be in hopeful anticipation for the next turn in the page.

--- a message from the Wisdom Tree

The Tree of the Knowledge of Good and Evil stood in a dark forest on a quiet evening. Even though it still held its fruit and the leaves were still green, it seemed dead without its blue radiance.

A slow crescendo of blue gathered around the tree, as someone was approaching. It was Evere's eyes that appeared in the thick of the trees. Since she had encountered the strange serpent, it was her first night back.

The two star-like eyes floated above the ground, close to the tree, without going all the way up to it. She was unsure if she was capable of seeing it again, as she closed her eyes to rehearse what the creature taught her. There was more than enough curiosity in her, as the blinding light surrounded her again. Glorious knowledge was at her disposal from the visionary windows at each branch.

The one closest to her caught her attention, as it showed what looked like a tree within a tree. From what she heard about the Tree of Life, this seemed to fit the description. The biggest landmark in the garden from what she saw.

The window focused on a different area that showcased a giant pool. Fruit was dropping into it and were floating towards land. When the first piece reached the shore, it miraculously changed into a black bear, as it walked away from view. She hoped to visit this other tree someday, but her fascination of the one she was at right now was sure to keep her coming back many more nights to follow.

There was another window she caught a glimpse into that captured a throne that sat a worthy king. His glory was so great; the earth was used as his footstool. Joy poured like rivers from his eyes, and his smile offered warmth to the lowly planet under his feet. Evere desired to serve a king like this. It was enough visions for one night, as she resigned back through the woods to be with Alphason.

**

A full day was enough time to wait to visit the tree again, as Evere returned the following night. She allowed herself to draw nearer to the tree that generously dispensed its knowledge, and chose to focus on a different branch that transported her imagination to another world. It looked like an endless domain that was dark but full of light, like a home for the stars she could only gaze at night. There were also what looked like giant-sized grapefruit suspended in mid-air, and some had rings around them. It must have been millions of miles away from here.

She wondered if the king knew of this place, as she located the branch from the previous night. It was unexpected for her to find the throne empty and wondered where the king could have gone. Her curiosity of this particular image grew mysterious from the disappearance. She decided to return again to see if the tree will offer a clue to his whereabouts. Where else would one go to for knowledge this confounding?

**

It was the night of the third visit where she discovered music that was unlike what the birds sang to her every day. She decided to go all the way up to the tree, so she could view a window that displayed a choir of angels. They were confusingly muted, as she attempted to touch the image. Her hand passed through it like water. The undulations activated a sound that was first quieter than a whisper, then grew loud enough to wake the entire forest. It was the most beautiful sound she had ever heard and the rivers of joy she saw flowing from the king's eyes now flowed through hers. Tears fell from her face, as it was something she had not felt before.

She furthered her investigation of the window that showed the empty throne. It had changed. A newborn baby, in a rough looking cradle made of wood, was displayed this time. Evere had never seen a human baby before, but it could hold the answer, as to where the king went. More examination was needed, as it prompted a reason to visit another night. She decided it was time for Alphason to share her experiences.

**

It was more like a week had passed until her next return. A trip to the Tree of Life kept her away, for a little while. She was without Alphason again, as she decided to go straight to the branch that showed the baby. She was astonished at what she saw. A woman was now holding it. Evere instantly knew the significance, as a decision was finally made, within her.

"There you are." Alphason had finally arrived, as his eyes wandered out of the forest, into the area she was at.

"I'm pleased you made it." Alphason began his study of the tree.

"I don't get it. Can one see something in a tree, while the other sees another?"

"You just have to know how to look. The serpent told me it was curiosity that brought out its knowledge. Can you close your eyes for me and do as I say? I will be for you, like the serpent was for me." He shuts his eyes and waits for instruction. "Imagine everything that the Word has shared with us and allowed us to experience, including everything that you know about me."

"I am. Isn't it wonderful that we don't have to imagine it, but actually experience it for ourselves?" Her eyes approached his eyes.

"Now imagine another side to me; one that you have never seen before."

"You can't imagine something you have never been a witness to."

"You are right, of course, which is why the tree will show you by opening your eyes, but be careful. It is much to take in at first." She had succeeded in opening up his curious nature, as the tree could now be experienced by both. When he adjusted his vision to the light, he looked upon the windows for the first time.

"The Word must be very busy to oversee all of this. Is there no end to his gifts?" Evere drew to the window of the woman and the baby.

"You see this? What would you suppose this is all about?"

"You have had more experience here. Maybe you can tell me."

"You see, the serpent told us that to experience what we see in the tree, we will have to eat its fruit."

"You know what the Word said."

"I do, but the serpent told us it was allowed, and the Word must have sent him. The creature revealed the future to me. He said that it was destined that one day we will eat from it."

"This must be a very wise creature to know such a thing."

"He said that the Word knows we will go through with it. Why put it off? You know who this child is? It is the Word, and she is his mother. The serpent explained to me that one day I will see something in this tree that I cannot do without. What better honor can there be for a woman than to be mother of the Word? Is there something you see in the tree that you must have?" Alphason found a window that showed a kingdom that held no time within its gates. It was a kingdom that would last forever.

"I wonder who is king of this place."

"It could be you. I'll be the mother of the Word, and you can be a king." She picked up a white pear that had fallen from the tree and gave it to Alphason. A blue apple was her fruit of choice, as she collected it from the ground. "Let's not avoid destiny any longer. Eternity can be a very long time to resist."

CHAPTER 17

Clash

From the depths of the Tree of Life, there was something that was unaccounted for, during Alphason's underwater excursion. It was wrapped around the roots of the tree, underneath the dirt, and sprouted from the ground into the giant pool. The hole that the whale passed through was where the chain led. Across the universe, with millions of intersections leading to unknown worlds, it eventually wound itself back to earth where it began. All those light years of metal, there was no vulnerability, other than the act of forbidden desire. For that will of disobedience, an enforcer was on its way like a comet, with its metal sharpened to exact precision. It was a sword for a new age to come.

The chain, leading back to earth, swayed, as a giant winged reptile with a protruding head had perched itself on top of it, high above the ground. It futilely tried to bite and peck at the link, underneath it. The sword was set ablaze with unquenchable fire when it reached the Earth's atmosphere and was on a direct collision course with the chain. The winged reptile escaped just in time before the metal clashed with metal. The chain was obliterated into thousands of tiny green particles, never to be one again. The sword carried on to another area of the garden, with unfinished business.

The winged reptile flew to the ground for another place to rest. It was one of many bound giants in the garden and was allowed a certain amount of freedom, unlike some. It was not allowed to drift too far away from the chain; that had recently broken.

The flyer found an area, just outside the forest that sheltered the Tree of the Knowledge of Good and Evil. The ground he rested on sloped downwards, leading to a lake. It was the same lake that held the reptile that mystified Evere the night of the encounter. It was no longer at a boil, and the water was uninhabited.

**

The sight of a flaming sword passing by above the trees was not enough to distract Evere and Alphason, who had just eaten from their selected fruit. They were disturbed at the nudity they saw before them. "Why do you show me yourself in such a way?" was the awkward question posed to Evere. They were no longer invisible and had no cloth. They were ugly to each other, out of shame, for what they did. A familiar voice called out.

"Good and evil can come from this." A sinister laugh followed the mocking. "Evil awaits, and I assure you good will only be a distant memory for you now."

"It sounds like the serpent," cried Evere. "Why does it taunt me now?"

"We should leave this place, quickly!" advised Alphason. He only made it a little far into the forest when he noticed Evere did not follow. A scream was heard, as Alphason turned around and noticed Evere was still in front of the tree. She stared at it in absolute horror. Alphason returned to her, in haste, and looked at the tree himself. Terrible visions were now at each branch of the tree. Death and unspeakable abominations were on display. Red was now the color in its fruit.

"What you now see in that tree is that wonderful child-king, murdered because of what you did," spoke the voice of the serpent.

"You tricked us!" accused Evere. "Why do you hide from us?"

"Who's hiding?" The moment he said this, they finally noticed the hundreds that were standing around them, scattered throughout the forest. They looked like men, who had become disturbed over time and wore white robes that did not seem to match their gloom. All of them were bald, except for one, who was standing closest to Alphason. He had an orange afro, holding a large white egg. "You will need to be the ones hiding. The Word is no longer an ally of yours, but an enemy. Don't worry. I will take care of you, as your new master."

"Why would we trust you? We will never come with you!"

"As if you had a choice." The New Word motioned one of his followers over. The one that responded, jumped on Alphason, bringing him to the ground. He savagely beat him, with his empty hand that didn't hold a feather, but still left his breath in him. Evere cried in anguish, pleading for him to stop.

"He's had enough pain to experience for his first time," ordered the New Word. The beating stopped, as the follower released him. Alphason could not get up from the agony he was in. "It is something you will have to get used to. The easy life is over. You two are my slaves now. I won you from your disobedience. As long as you do as I say, the pain will be kept to a minimum. You are no good to me dead, which, by the way, is unavoidable. The Word will no longer preserve your life. Death is your destiny now. I have something to show you."

He brought them towards the outland of the forest, where the land was flooded over by the nearby lake. They climbed over a small, scaly landmass, where they saw a pale carcass being washed over, on the other side. Its life force was being poured out, into the connecting stream. It was the behemoth that Evere loved so much. A depression formed in her, as her tears didn't come from joy anymore. "It was your sin that caused this. Not only did it allow the chain to release us, but" –

Before he could finish, water launched through the sky, like a canon, hitting the winged reptile, who was watching in the sky. The water scalded him, bringing him to the ground. The hot propulsive water originated from the mouth of the beast, as it emerged from the depths of the flood. It opened wide its mouth to the doomed flyer, as the more sensitive ones looked away from the violence displayed. The long slender neck was misleading, as it was attached to an enormous fat body. "The leviathan commands these waters. He will be exploring the river for a more fitting world that can fill his appetite. As long as you stay bound to me, these waters will not be trouble for you, for he is bound to me. He is one of many beasts that I have a say over. They are very dangerous to the ones that defy me. Because you are now my property, I will have dominion over this garden and everything in it."

He began to shout, so everyone in the forest and on the grassland could hear him. "Our business now is with the Tree of Life! We will go and lay claim to it! We have waited long enough and will begin our journey before the sun rises again!"

CHAPTER 18

A Different Way to Live

The sun was soon to rise. The New Word's caravan had already covered miles, as they followed the stream that would guide them to the Tree of Life. Evere and Alphason were kept at the front, close to their new master. So far, the Werd had kept his word on not getting too carried away, with pain that they were already feeling, from the rough ground they now walked upon. Alphason still felt the beating from earlier.

They felt heavier than they were used to, and sweat made them uncomfortable. Evere felt extra discomfort having no covering, among a multitude of what looked like men. She dreaded what it could be like when the sun would shine on her.

They overheard a conversation, between the Werd and one of his followers.

"...and the nights will be our time for travel."

"So we will need to make camp when the sun is ready."

"I do hate the sun, but I would like Evere and Alphason to experience it for the first time. They will learn to hate it, just like me." A roar is heard in the trees they were passing by. "Can it be?" A giant monstrous head appeared from the top of the trees that they could see from the river. It had rows of razor sharp teeth, in a mouth shaped like a grin. "It is my rex. Do you see it? That is what you will have to face if you try and separate from me. He has been waiting for quite a long time and is very hungry. Do we have an offering for him?" He asked one of the followers.

"Some of the others have located a horse," spoke a follower close by. "He is kept in the line a ways back. We thought he could become useful to you, so you would not have to walk all the way to the tree."

"Well, we must give him something. I can't let him down. He is my favorite, you see. You can find me another horse."

"As you wish, my Werd." This was the brown horse that provided adventure for the two humans. It was a fond memory for them both, as it was brought to the edge of the trees.

"No, not that one!" cried Evere.

"I see you are very fond of this horse," replied the Werd. "He is going to die anyway. It cannot be stopped."

"Can there be some other way?"

"The rex must be satisfied. The only way we can save this one is to find another in its place. If you can do this, then I will use this horse as my own escort."

"How can you ask of me to do this? How can I decide whose life to lose?"

"I will do it," offered Alphason. "I will find a replacement."

"Not on your own. Two of my followers will help you." Evere stared at Alphason, in disbelief.

"There is no other way. We made the choice when we ate from the tree, but I will not allow you to have to go through with this. The blood will be on my hands."

**

Alphason and the two followers searched the woods, on the other side of the stream from the rex. It was hours after midnight, as they attempted to find another sacrifice before the sun rose. It was easy enough to find, being a white horse. The harder part was keeping it from running off. "How do we trap it?" asked Alphason.

"It will have to be you to go up to it. There was a time when it trusted you. Maybe it still does." Alphason saw the two that were with him and noticed the paragons they were holding. One had what looked like a tail of an unknown, ungulate[6] creature, and the other had an igneous rock.

"When I bring it over, I don't want it eaten alive. We will kill it first. Find some more heavy rocks to bludgeon it."

"We will do as you say, but only because the New Word protects you. Otherwise, we would prefer to kill you instead." The horse was uncertain at first when it saw the naked man. Once it glimpsed the eyes it recognized, it became obedient to him. He was led to the others, with rocks placed in their hands. Alphason continued staring at its eyes, giving it comfort when it died. It was enough to make a grown man cry at the sight of crimson stained in the white coat.

**

It took six of the fallen to carry the carcass to the other side of the stream, where the rex was. They attempted to hurry for fear of being devoured by the monster, as well but managed to escape back to the line. They stared and waited, for the horse to be eaten, but wondered why the rex would not indulge, just yet. "What's the matter?" asked one of the followers. "Does it not like the horse?"

"I almost forgot," responded the New Word. "The rex doesn't like to be seen when it hunts. We can carry on. Our job is done here. My garden will have different needs than the old one. The animals you used to take care of will be food for my beasts. It is a different way to live. Someday you, yourself will be wondering what these animals will taste like. Curiosity has always been your downfall. We are nearly an hour before the sun. More ground needs to be covered before we stop. Bring me my new horse to ride upon."

**

As the sun crawled upon the landscape, followers bundled the New Word on his horse, with extra robes. He called out to Evere and Alphason, from underneath. "Where can you hide now? The Old Word is looking for you." The sun did not fill them with good-natured

---

6   Any members of a diverse clade of primarily large mammals that includes horses, cattle, pigs, giraffes, camels, deer, and hippopotamuses.

warmth anymore but was condemning, as it beat down on them, with its heated rays. The uncontrollable sweat made them very thirsty, and life just became more unbearable. The woman looked like she was about to faint, as Alphason tried to hold her. It was unwelcome to her, as she shrugged him away.

"Are you going to be okay?"

"I think I will die soon."

"I thought you said you would keep our pain lessened if we submit?!" accused the wearily angered human to the Werd.

"I had every intention of resting until sunset. I just wanted to have you experience the invasion, for the first time."

CHAPTER 19

Seed of Faith

The woods provided relief, from a blistering sun. Evere and Alphason were taken into a thickly covered area for rest, by a follower with a round mirror, who resented them greatly. The reflective shard was an obsession of his. It was cut so finely, it would slice the hand off of anyone that tried to steal it. He was very careful not to cause himself harm.

He couldn't look away from his own ugly reflection, as he spoke. "Now remember. That old life of yours is over. You've been spoiled, for far too long. None of us like you. Just give me a good reason to introduce you to death, by running. I will keep my eye on you, while the monsters in the woods will have two eyes glued to your every move. Some of them have four eyes. Others have eight legs..." the follower laughed, as he walked away.

As Evere and Alphason tried to get comfortable on the ground, the follower gave them some distance. He stayed close enough to see them. "Sleep will be a lot harder to achieve on this floor," said an irritated Alphason. "I never knew sticks and rocks can be so uncomfortable." Evere remained silent and repressive. "You're mad at me, for killing the animal. I'm glad you are. We should still hold on to the things that we value, but we will have to learn to adapt. The Word gave us dominion over these creatures. It is our say to what happens to them. Every life that is lost will go back to the Word, but in our case, we will return to the dust. You can be mad at me, just have some faith that I will help you through this. I will need your help as well."

"What about the Word? Why doesn't he help?"

"We broke his commandment. We are not entitled to his comfort anymore. If the Word is ever to help us, there will have to be complete humility and submission from us again."

"How are we to do that when we are slaves to the New Word, as he calls himself? We will die without him." Evere considered the wisdom of her words. "Oh, what's the use? We're going to die, anyway. I rather it is in the hands of freedom, than with that snake." She looked over to the follower. "You think he can hear us?"

"Are you thinking what I'm thinking?" he asked quietly. She nodded, with understanding. "It will have to be at the right moment. There are too many of them. We'll give it a couple of days, at least until we make it to the Tree of Life. Maybe hope lies within its reach."

"As I've said before, I'll follow you anywhere." She looked off towards a strange branch, where something seemed to be hanging off of it. "Do you see that?"

"Where?" It looked like two brown coats of animal skin.

"On that branch over there. That is not a feature of that tree." Alphason went over to it and unwrapped them off. "Do you think the Word left them there?"

"Who else could it have been? If he did, even the Word will take an animal's life in this age. I know what this is for. Here." He threw one over to Evere. "Put it on."

"You think?" She felt liberated at the thought of being covered up, as she slipped into it. "The Word still looks after us."

"Well, look at what you have there," interrupted the vain follower sarcastically, as he came back over. "Who gave you those?"

"Who do you think?"

"You think just because the Old Word made you a robe that he still loves you? How do you think we got these robes? I wouldn't be surprised if those things were poisoned."

"What does 'poisoned' mean?" Laughter came from the mocker.

"Boy, you too really are dumb. Poison is something that will prematurely bring an end to your lives if you ingest it, or come in contact with it in some way. You two need to get some rest. You have a long night ahead of you."

He returned to his post, as they tried to lay back down. Alphason felt around his coat, for fear of this poison, and located a small compartment on his right hip. He put his hand inside and came out with a handful of seed. Evere watched the events unfold. "What is the seed for?"

"The Word intended on us to find it."

"Should we plant it?"

"What if its poison?" They looked at each with dread, from fear of being out of the care of the Word. They were uncertain, as to how wrathful he was. "We should probably wait until we have further knowledge of what it does." Alphason returned the seed back in the pocket. "Let's try and get some sleep on this ground we will return to someday."

As they attempt to sleep through their discomfort, Evere became aware of two eyes in the midst of the woods. "There is something watching us. There should be a name for something that can blend in with its environment."

"And what's that?"

"I don't know, but we shall have to think of one. Maybe we could learn its secret so we can stay hidden from the monsters and the New Word, or is it the Old Word that we should be afraid of? Maybe death is something to look forward to."

CHAPTER 20

Flaming Sword

By the second night, the stream was deep enough to sink a child and was waist-deep for the average sized participant of the journey. There was a cool breeze facilitated, by the water they walked beside. Everyone got a good glimpse of the miles ahead of them to see what's in store for them, as the ground began to drift downwards into a long hill. The land still had much beauty to it, because many of its thorns and monsters were hidden as a trap, for those who are unsuspecting.

When they reached the bottom of the hill, the climb atop another hill began for the restless. It was just as long as the one leading down. The ascent became easier, as they were all fixated at a luminescence over the top of the apex. They were astonished to find another fallen, who they had an understanding were all within the ranks of their group. Scattered ones were not foretold by the New Word. The man was standing in the middle of the shallow river, looking up towards the sky. They didn't know what he was looking at, but they were enchanted by a golden radiance, coming off of him. He also had gray hair on his head, which made them all suspect the Old Word was up to something.

"You there," hollered the Werd, with a chain in his hand. It had the same color of the brilliance surrounding the stranger. "Have you a moment to share with us news of the former Word?" The man would not speak, as he pointed towards the sky. "We see nothing up there, you fool. There is leviathan that haunts this river. You may not want to be in there for very long."

"Fire," spoke the man ominously. The golden radiance began to weaken, as his hair started to fall out.

"What is this you speak of?" He would not explain himself. Fire was all that he would mutter.

"Seize him and get him to speak," ordered the Werd. They obeyed, as they brought him back in the ranks, without a struggle. One of the followers, who held a dead tarantula, approached the Werd.

"We could not get him to talk. He doesn't know his name, or where he came from, and seem to be even dumber than these two over here." He was referring to Evere and Alphason. "He will be easy to control. You will not have to worry about him."

"Then let's continue on."

Others were found on that second day in the river. Each of them with only one thing on their mind; a fire they could not explain, as they stared into the heaven.

**

The third night met with the longest hill, yet. Evere and Alphason got the worst of it, for lack of conditioning. They were almost there, as evident by the river that would drown any man, and was too far to cross for the strongest swimmer. By the two's earlier recollection from their previous visit to the tree, this hill they were on was probably the last.

In their attempt at an escape, the two humans managed to mix their way backward in the line, oblivious to the Werd. If there were to be any chance of separation, they would have to get lost in the crowd. They were still stuck out like a sore thumb, due to their brown skins in a sea of white robes.

When the top of the hill was reached, the line ahead of them halted. They were staring at the world in front of them. "What are they looking at?" asked Alphason to anyone who would listen. "Is it the Tree of Life they see?"

One of the followers, who was at the front of the line, emerged into the ranks where they were. He had a darker epidermis than the rest and seemed to carry news with him, along with a small page from an unknown book. "They see the tree, along with something else."

"Are we in for a new wonder?" asked one of the followers.

"It is still too far to make out what it is. It looks to be a wild kind of light, we have never seen before, in front of the tree where the pool is."

"Why are we not moving?"

"The master wants volunteers to go and investigate before the rest of us move onward. Do we have anyone whose will is with the New Word?"

"Me and Evere will go," volunteered Alphason. Evere looked at him with a quizzical look. "This could be our moment," he whispered.

"Well, we'll see," responded the follower. "I doubt he'll let you two go alone. Come with me."

**

It was a company of ten, counting Evere and Alphason, who traveled on the other side of the hill, towards the tree they could view. It was only level ground from here.

The light was very much alive that they could see in the distance but was still too far to see exactly what it was. The river flowed from the giant pool and was still canopied, by the looming branches. Nothing seemed to be out of the ordinary, other than the light. The tree was still growing, providing life to the region. "Maybe this is the fire the stranger was talking about?" suggested Alphason.

"You do not know anything," said a stubborn follower with pale skin, who was holding a small brown book that appeared to have some pages missing. "He was looking to the sky as his reference."

"Maybe that is where it came from?"

"That fool didn't know anything, and you're just about as dumb for listening to him."

The rest of the multitude behind them started to advance when they were convinced the ground the smaller party had already traveled upon was safe. When the ten made it to the giant pool, a tool with sharpened precision was surrounded by the wild light they could now recognize. It was suspended in mid-air, gripped by an invisible force, just above the center of the water. The size of the metal perceived to have colossal dimensions.

"How will we know if it is safe?" asked Evere.

"He'll lead the way," proposed the pale follower, pointing at Alphason.

"Me?"

"I only wish. I was referring to the one coming down the river behind you." The head and back of the leviathan was seen, swimming upstream in the river, towards the giant pool. "Looks like he found a new home. Think of all the animals that spawn from this place he can indulge in. He'll be quite the big one before too long."

The monster entered the pool and swam around the front a little bit before it explored the other side. When it crossed the center, the wild light that enveloped the metal lit up the leviathan underneath. The wildness that was encircling him did not seem to bother him, as he continued his fascination of the pool. A white beluga whale, who had gone up for air, was discovered on the other side, as the beast zeroed in and attacked it.

"This injustice cannot go on forever," uttered Alphason.

"Why worry? He probably won't come after us, with all these creatures distracting him. As you can see, he was not harmed. It is safe to pass." The company carried on, but Evere and Alphason lagged behind. They were still uncertain, as they studied the leviathan. The water that pulsated from its mouth was also surrounded by the fire that Alphason was convinced was its name. The beast was aiming at birds in the sky and various creatures that were on land. They, however, did not seem to survive the fire. Evere and Alphason froze, as they called out to the other eight.

"I would not go any farther if I were you."

"You're stupidity makes you afraid."

**

The New Word and the multitude found a good spot in front of the pool to view the progress of the advancement. "The Old Word has kept this knowledge from me. He is selfish to not pass it on. This is my world now. How dare he intrude on it."

"Master, the group seems to be moving on without two of them," shared a follower, with a spyglass he peered through. "It must be Evere and Alphason."

"I told them not to leave the two. What are they--"

Before he could finish, the eight that went ahead were lit up by the fire. The sound that carried over was screaming. Evere and Alphason observed to be running away.

"They are suffering! What are we to do?!" The multitude behind them was becoming unhinged, like they were going to retreat.

"Stay where you are! There is another way around!" The moment after the New Word shouted this, the invisible force that held the metal suspended in the sky had lifted. It dropped and crashed into the water. A tidal wave of fire was created, sweeping the ground around it. An uncontrollable fire spread into the areas surrounding the tree, guarding anyone of entry. The hundreds behind the New Word became convinced the fire was going to spread to where they were, as retreat became an afterthought to their running.

Some loyal followers decided to stay with the New Word. "Let them go! There are too many of them! Evere and Alphason must not get away, however! Go find them!" The followers were reluctant but did what they were told, as they traveled to the fiery ground.

From the New Word's vantage point, the fire seemed to have consumed much and became more distressed at what was about to happen next. "He wouldn't dare!" The fire was leading to the Tree of Life itself and did not divert when it reached it. Within minutes, the fire had spread to the tips of the looming branches, as the tree tilted and collapsed into the pool.

CHAPTER 21

Despair Seen Through the Eyes of Hope

Evere and Alphason were hoping to use this opportunity to escape, but survival had become the number one priority. The wild was everywhere around them. They were untouched by the flame but were close enough to it to feel its overpowering heat. It was dizzying and became harder to fill their lungs with fresh air. Coughing was an unwelcome feeling for their first time. Every direction they looked seemed to be a dead end, or it could have just seemed that way, due to a world that was growing hazy.

Evere had trembled to the ground, bringing her husband down with her. They had not the strength to get back up again. Alphason decided to use what was left of his weakened voice. "Forgive us, Word. You are our first love. With my last breath, I will only serve you." Before the world faded, he could have sworn there were two eyes that stared at him through the fire.

**

The fire would not take them, just yet. Evere had woken in the middle of a grassland that was a safe distance from the inferno. The other was still unconscious but seemed to be breathing beside her. She heard voices that sounded like followers. "They couldn't have gone far!" was what she heard, as she tried to wake Alphason.

"Get up! We have to keep moving!" Alphason started to revive, as he rose his back from the ground.

"What happened?"

"We are safe for now, but not for long. The followers are looking for us. We have to keep pushing."

"Let's head towards the river, so we won't get lost. There are too many monsters in the woods." They hurried to the river and began running, along its edge. The followers sounded like they were right behind them.

"We'll have to go into the woods. They'll find us by the river."

"There is another option. They are all only on one side of this river. If we swim to the other side, they'll never find us over there. The leviathan should be either dead, or preoccupied with the giant pool. He shouldn't bother us. We used to swim these rivers."

"Then what are we waiting for?" Evere entered the pool, as Alphason followed. One thing they were not ready for, other than the wide length of the river, was that there was a strong current that pushed them further in the garden. Alphason noticed that Evere was dragging behind him.

"What's the matter? You used to be a faster swimmer than me." Great fatigue set in once they reached the center. "We'll never make it. It's too far, and it's the same distance either way. We should have never attempted this. It's all my fault we are out here. It was my brilliant idea."

When he looked behind him to see Evere's progress, she was gone. He assumed the worst. "No!!! Why couldn't I save you?" He himself was at the end of his strength, as the world started to fade again, but not until he got another glimpse of the eyes. They were staring at him, again, at the top of the water, he was sinking beneath.

**

By morning, the river would also not offer a final resting place, for the two that lay horizontal on the bank. They had managed to make it to the other side. Life was still offered to them, as they breathed an unconscious breath.

The one that was first to animate was Alphason, as he lunged up. He stretched his eyes to the other side of the river and wondered how he managed to survive. There were no followers that he could see, from where he sat. The sun was more tolerable than it was. It was enough for him to be grateful for the circumstances. "Unbelievable" was a word that was not used by him before, until now. There were giant tracks around him, but he could not make out what they belonged to. "You need to get up. It's a wonderful morning," he tried to communicate to Evere.

When she finally emerged from her sleep, she had a somewhat different, more cynical reaction to the day. "I believe I heard you say it was a wonderful morning."

"It is. We're still alive, and the followers are absent." This seemed to cheer her up a bit.

"I suppose it is a good thing."

"It's even better when you consider that it must have been the Word that saved us. This sun doesn't seem so bad now, does it?"

"I guess you're right."

"The New Word hates the sun, only because of his hatred for the Old Word. There's no reason that we should share in his misery. So what do you think we should do now?" Her response was by slapping him. "What was that for?"

"I don't know. For some reason, I had this irresistible urge to do that. Did you forget something?"

"I don't believe so."

"The seed. Do you still have it?" A thrill shot through his body at the thought.

"Oh yeah." He reached into his pocket for the gift that was given to them. His mood immediately sunk when he pulled out his empty hand. "It's not there anymore."

"Where could it have gone? Search the ground! It must be somewhere!" They scanned the immediate area around them before a thought occurred to Alphason that completely broke him. He sat with a glazed look.

"It must have flushed out in the river."

"There's no way we will ever find it in that! All hope is lost!" They both moped on the ground, as they tried to think of any other possible solution.

"There is another thing we can do."

"And what could you possibly say that could bring my hope back to me?"

"Maybe we can have a child." Evere immediately stood up and began walking off down the river, as Alphason tried to follow her. "What's the matter?"

"The reason I did not wake up in as good of a mood as you this morning was because *that* was what I saw!" She pointed towards the Tree of Life, which they still had a good view of. The tree and its land around it were completely blackened from the fire. Its life was gone and was replaced with smoke. "The Tree of Life is gone forever. How long do you think we have until the rest of this land dies with it?"

"There is still water in the pool and the rivers. It may be a very long time before everything is dried up."

"What would be the point of bringing a child into this world? There will be no future for it. When we die, so must our legacy." Alphason stood in deep contemplation, refusing to give up.

"There is one last thing we could do."

"I've had enough false hope, Alphason. Just let me die in my grief."

"Just hear me out. We make another journey to the Tree of Knowledge. Maybe there is still some good left in that tree. Maybe there is something that we have missed that could give us an answer, as to what to do next."

"I do not have the heart to look at that tree anymore."

"You do not have to look. I'll look. Will you come with me? Please, don't give up on me yet." She walked back to Alphason, as she took his hands.

"I'll follow you once again."

**

Staying close to the river allowed them to see whatever monster wanted to drink, but they knew it would not work once a beast picked up their scent. A full day had passed without an attack, as they wondered if their safety on their journey was being provided, by the Old Word.

They had a weird sense as if they were being followed. Periodically, they would see eyes in the trees that would never come out of hiding. Evere tried to make contact with it the second evening. "I see you. Are you afraid of us? You don't seem like you want to eat us." She felt like a fool when a turkey emerged from the woods to get drink from the river. "This one will not last long. So many things out there, wanting to eat it." A grumbling was heard in her stomach. "I'm getting hungry myself." Alphason stared at her, curiously. "No. I am not ready to do such a thing. We just need to find some fruit, but I am afraid if we stray away from this river, we might not return."

"Once we get to the tree, there will be fruit to eat. It's just a couple of more days till we get there." They learned that it was better to travel during the day. It was nice to see where they were going, and they were able to cover more ground that way.

**

The third evening an inexplicable wind picked up suddenly, but they had not any evidence as to what caused it. The wind died down as quickly as it started, and they decided there was no reason for alarm. They safely arrived, as they came within the outskirts of the forest that hid the tree. The two stopped, before they entered, when noises were heard from within. "Do you hear that?"

"Do you think it is the New Word?"

"There were others that got separated that I was able to witness from the fiery fields. Some of them may have returned here as well. It is a big risk going in there, but we have to get to the tree. I usually ask for you to come with me. As I promised, you will not have to see its knowledge. This time, I will go alone. Stay out here and wait for me."

"If that is what you wish."

"I do not wish to ever to have to separate from you, but I would rather have you live longer than me if it comes down to it. I will return. The grass is long here. If you lie down, they may not see you." She did just that, as he entered the forest.

He followed the unknown noise, as he rationalized it probably originated close to the tree. The closer he approached, voices became clearer. Once he reached the outer circle, he knelt behind a fallen tree. He hoped it would offer enough cover.

He felt he was not alone in the woods. It was like there was something else very close to him. Whatever it was seemed like it was trying to hide, as well.

Followers or deserters were within view. He could not conclude to what loyalty they belonged to. The tree he could also see, but the visions were still too far for him to make out.

"Bring her here," ordered one of the followers, who was of strong build. Alphason became unnerved, as he became sober to what he was referring to. Evere was pushed into the inner area, by the unsympathetic fallen. "Where is the other?" was the question before the hulk slapped her, with a hand that held a black claw, scarring her face.

"Get your filthy condemned hands off of her!" cried Alphason, as he darted away from his hiding spot. There were too many of them, as the others swarmed and tackled him to the ground.

"It was a good thing you came out when you did," declared the one that slapped her. "Because you don't want to know what I was going to do next to her. Bring him over to me." The ones that kept him down on the ground brought him over, as they stood him next to Evere. She did not seem as white hot with anger as Alphason was. In fact, she looked to be thrilled about something. Her eyes were directed to the tree.

"What are you looking at?" whispered Alphason.

"Quiet!" interfered the dominant follower. "The New Word knew you would return to this tree. Many say you two are not very intelligent. I see that they were right. The master would like to see you now." As they ushered them away, Alphason tried to penetrate further, as to what Evere had witnessed.

"There is still good in that tree," was all that she would share. When they reached the place where the New Word was, it looked much like the ground that Evere encountered the serpent the first night. This one, in comparison, had a tall spiral hill that allowed a moon to haunt its ground, with its wicked light. It was a place where it was possible to see over the tops of the trees. The evil one stood on top of the hill, looking off to a sky that held no wonder for him. There was a spyglass in his hand he would not use.

"You two must be starving," he surmised, with his back to them. "Eat". Food was brought to them. There were some fruit, and raw meat of unknown variety was offered. "You will not be as strong as you can be in this life if you don't eat something that doesn't grow from the ground. My followers and I were able to make it to this tree faster than you because we eat the strength of others. But if you are not ready to try it yet, you may have what you are comfortable with."

"We will have neither. We do not serve you anymore. The Word still protects us." The New Word winced at his statement but would not allow them to see his vulnerability, with his back turned. "We had almost died twice since we were away from you, but somehow we survived. The first time we were pulled out of the fire. The second we almost drowned in the river but found ourselves on the bank, by morning." The Werd started to laugh. "What do you think is so funny? The fact that we do *not* need you anymore? The whole time we were traveling on our way back to this tree, we weren't even attacked by one beast. Who do you think provided us with a safe path?" The New Word turned around and offered a kind smile, which left them a little unprepared.

"Only to wind up back here under the authority of me. It was me that kept the beasts away from you. It was my followers that pulled you out of the fire and the river."

"Then why did you not capture us then?"

"What would be the point? I predicted that you would return here. You see, it was a part of my plan to show you what life would be like without me. You nearly died twice, and you return to me half-starved. You are not aware of this, but Evere has been crying in anguish, since she was captured and brought to me. She is sick. This is what happens when you go without food for too long. It feels like your insides are spilling to the ground. You have not been able to take care of her like I can. Stop making demands you cannot keep. Don't let her starve any longer. Now eat!" The food was offered again, as Alphason grabbed a strawberry and gave it to Evere."

"I had no idea," said a worried Alphason.

"It's okay." They began to eat the fruit that was offered. Their heads were lowered, for the shame they felt.

"I told you I would take care of you," continued the Werd. "I never wanted to be cruel to you, but you leave me no choice. Because of what you two did, you will now have to be separated. I have jobs for both of you that will keep you away from each other. You will never see each other, ever again."

The horrible words spoken to them would have crushed them, which it did for Evere. Alphason, however, had caught a glimpse of a set of eyes, staring at him from above the trees, behind the New Word. The words of the false prophet seemed hollow to him, for it seemed the truth was not on his side.

CHAPTER 22

Ghost in the Desert

What was it that the fallen sand wanted to forget? Each of them held onto something that came from a world they have lost all memory of. These paragons-of-past were not items they kept in hopes of remembering the past. They were keys for building a future where they may be free of their creator.

The truth was not on their side, because it was something that was in direct conflict with the core of their nature. The truth was also hard to accept for the first man and woman. There was a part of them that wanted to forget and accept the amnesia that is a common characteristic of the sand. They preferred to allow the haunting memory of the fall linger in their consciousness, in fear of what they may turn into. The chance of ever reuniting with a vengeful Word may not seem like the best idea, but it was better than whatever the New Word had for them.

They thought they had the last accurate account of a perfect garden, untouched by impurity. There was something they missed. It was overlooked due to many distractions. The song that was played on Evere's third visit to the Tree of Knowledge had a power to it she did not perceive. It was loud enough to wake the entire forest and it reached the ears of the one they were to call Ghost.

It was a quiet evening before the song played. The gray dog stood very still, as he growled at a bizarre lizard with bulging eyes. It shared the same color of the gray rock it stood on. Ghost had very little trust in reptiles, big or small, and this one seemed even more deceptive than the serpent.

When he ran up to it, it vaulted down to the grass, as its gray skin changed to green. It scampered off into the forest where Evere had gone into to visit The Tree of the Knowledge of Good and Evil. It was her third consecutive night, but the dog kept his distance. He thought his use would be better suited going after various reptiles that could pose a threat.

He disliked going into the forest and decided to wait on the grassland. It kept its eyes glued to the trees, to see where a reptile might hide. A beautifully harmonic sound came from somewhere within, as it calmed the protective nature of the dog. It made him very sleepy, hearing the soothing sound, for it had been many days since he had slept. He had to rest sometime. Now seemed as good a time as any.

**

When the dog woke, it was morning. He had almost missed the departure of Evere and Alphason. They were traveling down the stream towards their first visit of the Tree of Life and weren't too far ahead to where he couldn't catch up. He was still yawning off his sleep, as he hurried along after the invisible humans.

It was a particularly joyful morning, as the dog still remembered the singing the night before. The song lived in him and made him feel like he could experience every goodness the garden had to offer. It tempted him to stop a couple of times to catch glimpses of the nature life around him, but he never let the humans get too far ahead. The shine that was casting off of their invisible forms was still easy to see from a great distance.

A butterfly was unaware of a race it was in with the dog down the river. The protector wished he could be up there with it, flying around as well. It reminded him of the chameleon he found earlier and believed he would learn its secret someday.

**

The dog had never knew how to swim before, as he stood at the edge of the giant pool. Evere and Alphason had already entered into it and were swimming towards its center. He wanted to follow in after them but was unsure how it was done. If he were to learn the secrets of the animals he marveled after, he would have to try new things. If the fish could do it, or the humans, then so could he, as he jumped in without the slightest clue how this was going to work.

His eagerness was not enough to keep him afloat, as he sank almost immediately. The threat of death was not a problem. It was just figuring out the trick to making it to the top again. He attempted to wield his legs as a fin but learned that would only work for the fish. To the bottom was where he found himself.

A decision was made to calm down and not force the issue. The melody was what he needed, as he allowed himself to remember. There was a rhythm to it as well, as he tried to match it by paddling with his legs. This seemed much more effective and began lifting himself from the bottom. It allowed the water to cycle around him to where he could push himself upward, and soon found himself at the top again.

The rhythmic paddling also helped him to stay afloat, as he learned his place in the world. It was above the water where he belonged. His knew talent of swimming would prove to be helpful in the coming future.

**

It was a very eventful trip to the Tree of Life, as everyone found their way back to the forest that felt like a home to them. Midnight had passed over. Evere had gone inside to visit the tree again. He witnessed Alphason going inside after her but decided to stay behind.

He was distracted by the lake at the bottom of the hill. It was a place he never explored before. Swimming was something that needed practice. He felt it may give him an advantage over the reptiles, by being adaptive.

He didn't notice the boiling until he was within a foot from entering into it. It was too dark too see it until now. The lake wasn't as wide as the pool at the Tree of Life, but it was big enough to give the feeling of how deep it could go. A waxing moon was reflecting off the surface, which helped illuminate the area. Growing fear in him came when he noticed no animals were anywhere near the banks. There wasn't anything he could see in the water, either, other than the bubbles that were quietly bursting on top.

He calmed himself when he saw the green-glowing chain on the other side of the lake. It was surfacing from the water, leading towards the forest. There was something foul underneath he was certain of, but the Word was aware of the evil that existed.

As he trotted back up the hill, he didn't see the humans at the top. It did not trouble his spirit. His sense of peace brought the music again, as it swept over his mind. This made him tired, as he decided to sleep off his adventure.

**

The dog enjoyed his new found skill in swimming, but the feeling of being wet was not a pleasant one, as he woke half buried in water. It was still dark out, but the ground he was lying on was flooded over by the nearby lake. He noticed that the lake itself had lost much of its level from the flood and the water he was in felt unusually warm.

The lake was even streaming through the forest, as he set his path towards this change in topography. He was unaware of the other presence until the run-off he was in started to bubble fiercely. Something was looming over him, he sensed. A burn was becoming unbearable and was his main area of concern. He needed to find relief from the boiling, as he searched the area around him. A floating log was nearby, as he desperately crawled onto it.

The dog turned and faced up to the leviathan. He almost couldn't see his long slender neck, because it was difficult to see past his huge belly. Its color on its stomach was a lighter blue compared to the rest of him. It did not seem to notice him because it was facing the pale behemoth that had fallen into a never-ending sleep, in the flood. Red was pouring out of the gentle giant, and its significance escaped the dog for it had never seen this before.

The leviathan dove underneath the shallow flood the best he could with his fat body and lied very still, hoping to be confused for a small landmass. Its back was very scaly, but wasn't as sharp as it looked.

The dog finally remembered to bark at it, for it remembered this kind of tactic his first adversary used on him when it tried to pretend to be dead. Poking its head above the water, the leviathan tried to pinpoint where the barking was coming from. Even though the dog stood right in front of it, the beast could not see him.

Voices in the woods were drawing near, as the monster buried his head underneath the water again. The boiling ceased, but the dog wasn't ready to come off of his log, just yet. It seemed like this new deceiver wasn't interested in harming the ones that were coming.

It was Evere, Alphason and hundreds of white-robed human-like beings that surrounded the area. The dog sensed an unusual amount of misery in everyone's faces around him. None of them could detect the leviathan yet and seemed unaware of what was right in front of them. The dog couldn't fully understand why no one could see him, but wondered if he somehow learned the trick of the chameleon. He decided to use this advantage by staying very quiet and figured this would be used better to protect his humans.

**

He had come to the conclusion that Evere and Alphason were under an unusual amount of stress than usual and believed that these men they were with were very dangerous. It seemed the day finally arrived for what his protective nature was really meant for, as he followed the multitude to the Tree of Life. There were too many of these nasty individuals and he would have to choose his moment wisely if he were to ever interfere.

Along with the leviathan and the rex he saw, there were many other dangerous-looking giants he saw in the woods. His small size seemed impotent in offering any real help if any of these monsters were to come after the two humans.

The music he loved accompanied him on his trip, and after a couple of days found that the giants in the woods did not seem as big as they used to be. It seemed strange that it was more difficult now to get a drink from the river. He had to bend his neck down further to make it work. It finally hit him when the New Word happened to walk obliviously by that his size was no longer an issue in thwarting unwelcome beasts. He was now considered a giant to the average-sized human.

The rest of the multitude were following the New Word, and he could see Evere and Alphason were still surviving. The line halted, as they reached the top of a long hill. Everyone was distracted at the visual on display over it. The dog was ready for anything and wondered if this was the time to make his presence known.

**

The sword had dropped, and chaos erupted. Ghost's presence had remained a secret, but it was time for interference. Though his might was growing, fire was still a considerable threat and it caused him to lose sight of his humans.

Within reach of the pool, a much-needed thought occurred. He wondered what would happen if water interacted with the fire and tried brushing a little of it onto a nearby flame, with his feet, to see what it would do. It miraculously snuffed it out.

There was an advantage of having an enormous head, as he filled his mouth with water, without swallowing. He reckoned this would be more efficient to put out more flame. It worked as it created a workable path towards the humans he now saw and believed it was the first time the man finally saw him.

When Ghost finally reached the two, he feared it was too late. There was still subtle movement in them and decided to use his advantage again. He fitted them into his mouth and crouched for a great leap.

There was too much distraction from the fire, as he tried to remember the song. He wasn't sure if he was ready, and the extra weight he had in his mouth created doubt. The fire had spread again and there wasn't access to any more water. The doubt may have been there, but he was without options.

He extended his legs and decided that if he were to jump he better herald it with a run. As he backed up, with the room he had left, he felt like gulping from being nervous. It was a thought that was quickly shelved, due to there being humans inside his mouth.

The fire was high and his heart was full. His legs were ready as the music began. A rhythm reached his feet, as they began to move. He began matching his speed with a crescendo and his jump synched with the melody.

It may have felt like flying to him. Granted, it was enough to keep his feet from touching the flame. He rose high enough to see the pool he was arching towards. The song was very complex and would lead him to descend. It was enough to escape the fire, as he dove into the depths.

He nearly plummeted to the bottom, but it only felt that way. He knew what to do from this point. His trusty dog-paddling skills was a skill he had already learned.

**

The humans proved to be troublesome. As soon as he brought them to the reaches of safety, they were just as quick to find danger again when they escaped into the river. The dog followed in after them and discovered the deep river wasn't deep for him. He was able to keep his head above the water, with his feet on the rocky bottom.

He reached an unconscious Evere, as he bowed his head underneath her body to carry her. It was effective to aide her to the other side of the river.

Alphason was next but had floated a ways, due to the strong current. He had sunken below the water before the dog had reached him. Unlike Evere, however, the man was still conscious, as he stared up at him through the water. His eyes closed before the dog cradled him inside his mouth.

By the time the dog had reached the shore, Alphason had passed out. No water had entered their lungs. The two were still breathing, as the dog relaxed next to them to regain his strength. He observed a search party of followers on the other side, but they had not a clue as to where the humans had fled. The dog had a feeling that his next test will be his toughest yet.

**

It was a very long three days, following the humans back to the Tree of the Knowledge of Good and Evil. The monsters in the woods were very interested in Evere and Alphason. They seemed too numerous to take care all of them.

The first day three reptilian giants were tracking the humans but were unaware that the dog was tracking them. His ability to blend in with his environment allowed him to get close enough to attack before they realized something happened to them. The dog's teeth felt stronger than they have ever felt and proved to be an effective weapon.

**

Five beasts hunted the humans the second day. It may have been more, but it was still easy enough for the dog to handle. One challenge presented itself when some of them were not as big as the rex. The traveled way below the trees and were harder to see. They still had a scent to them that Ghost was able to pick up. Raptors they were called and carried themselves like the rex. They were low-roaming bipedal[7] monsters who had the ability to move at a relentless speed.

A raptor seemed interested in a turkey that was searching the ground for its own food. There were many things in the world the turkey had to fear. Ghost was one of them and had found it first. It became a much-needed meal for him, now that he had a larger appetite he was not used to.

As he carried it away inside his camouflaged mouth, the raptor wondered how the turkey had disappeared. It was still searching the ground for what happened to the game before the dog came back over and finished him off.

**

It was easy enough to take care of the monsters that walked the ground, but the dog found his weakness were the predators that could fly. Dactyls they were called; winged reptiles who used their advantage above the ground to find their prey. Protruding heads and wings like bats were characteristics they shared. There were three of them on the third day, but it seemed he was too unprepared for this test to reach

---

[7]   An organism moves by means of its two rear limbs or legs.

Evere and Alphason before the flyers. The dactyls were nearly a mile away before they could reach the two humans.

A longer walk was for Ghost after he had been led by a fierce rex far into the forest. It was a trail that he had lost and it took him far from where he was supposed to be. Unfortunately, he had forgotten how the helpful song had went, as its melody had drifted to the back of his mind.

The sun was beginning to set as the dog searched the darkest part of the sky for the first star to appear. He heard a bell he believed was coming from within a northern part of the forest. It was a direction he was uncertain he should head, because his humans were still in the south. The dog wanted to investigate, but decided it will have to wait until he saw the first star for the evening.

When he finally spotted the first night light, he believed the bell that was ringing would give him his next indication on to what to do. As he walked towards the trail of sound, he was unaware of the giant of giants standing in the forest behind him with his bare back turned. The deliverer waited for the winged reptiles to fly into his direction. He had no covering and felt no shame. His long brown hair was long enough to cover his lower backside. The head reached to the top of the sky, and his hands were stretched out to the east and west. The sky had lost its sun for the evening, as thousands of stars were from the direction he was standing in.

Right when the birds got close enough to him, he spun around fast enough, creating a twister. He grabbed hold of them in his massive hands. The flyers were thrown out, like a comet to the ground.

The sound of the bell blew away with a wind that was leading further north and the trail was lost. Sensing that the ghost was alone again, he abandoned his walk. When he turned around, there was no other presence in the forest with him. At least what he could see from above the trees.

The sky held possibilities but no answers for him. He searched the stars for wings that weren't there but located a scent on the ground that led to what he was looking for. The flightless dactyls held no breath when he reached them. They were broken and buried underneath a thick gathering of trees that were rooted deep and would take a lot to knock down. There was no more to see here, as he rushed back to the humans that were now miles away in the south.

When he finally caught up with them, Evere and Alphason had entered into the forest that held the Tree of the Knowledge of Good and Evil. They managed to succeed in getting themselves captured again, as the dog watched them over the forest. He saw the man staring at him again when he was before the New Word and wondered why it was Alphason that always spotted him.

There was a tree here whose roots weren't as strong. It had fallen next to his paw and a suspicious feeling arose in him that things were going to change around here. He wondered what new colors he would have to blend in with to adapt to this new season. The desert was already here.

CHAPTER 23

Time in Eternity

Evere is virtuous not to abandon the injured white bird who crashed into the tree. It is her only companion in her isolated state. She looks to have been telling stories, as she is kneeling down and petting its back. Even though it is broken, it is soothed by her voice. "It was the last time I ever saw him. We were in that dying world for over five hundred years. Much had changed in that time, and I never got a chance to tell him what I witnessed in the tree. The child that was slain, somehow, came back to life."

She stands up and looks to the wintry world ahead of her hoping to see Alphason again. She puts her fingers through the gray streak in her hair, as she continues her story. "Death will still come to me eventually. In those five hundred years, the rivers were drying up, and a desert began forming in places that weren't close to a water source. The New Word stayed close to the Tree of Knowledge, for that ground was the greenest in the land. There were others that deserted when the Tree of Life fell and chose to remain scattered. They survived on the few patches of forest that were left. The New Word believed they would eventually try to come back when their forests died off...."

True to the New Word's promise, he had found jobs for Evere and Alphason that kept them away from each other. Evere was the master gardener and was tending a crop of vegetables. Followers kept watch over her, but she enjoyed being out here away from the New Word.

She was growing tired, as she sat in the dirt for a break when the sun began to set. The coat she wore was still the one given to her by the Old Word. The New Word offered her one made by him, but she refused. The one she had had proved to stand the test of time.

When she tried to get back up, the coat snagged on a thorn and ripped open a small tear in her side. She became frustrated, but a thought occurred to her, as she reached inside her new pocket. A handful of seed was what she pulled out in her hand. She saw that the follower, with a root in hand, wasn't looking as she immediately planted it in the ground.

"The New Word wants to see you and hear about your day," the follower yelled, with a voice that almost sounded like an angel. It was something that reminded her of how great her fall was.

"I'm coming," she said, as she got up.

The follower took her to the area with the spiral hill where a line was leading to the New Word. He was gripping a black claw. Evere saw this and remembered the scarring she was given from the brute follower who captured her.

When she became the next person in line, the New Word seemed very pleased. "So what can we expect from our crops soon?"

"We shall have beans."

"What kind of beans?"

"Green beans. Brown beans. Yellow beans and many others."

"So many to choose from. You may ask me anything you like."

"It has been a very long time since I have seen my husband. Is he alright?" The New Word seemed annoyed at first but used his smile again.

"You may ask me this question. Alphason is stronger than ever. He leads my searchers who explore the dying world to find anything of hope or news to bring back. He is out right now on a very important mission."

Ghost was watching them in the woods, with his green coat. He looked away through eyes that were now covered by untrimmed hair. From where he stood, he also could see Alphason and some followers walking along what was left of the stream. They were told to revisit the Tree of Life for something that may have survived the fire and make detours to the other forests. They were to compel the deserters to join with the New Word again.

As they followed the stream that was moist at best, the dog tried to catch up. They reached an area that was mostly sand, so the dog's coat changed to yellow. Alphason was also changing. A little gray was showing in his hair. He became wiser in his survival skills to go with it. Indulging in the flesh of animals was still a taboo to him.

The farther the searchers travelled down the stream, the more water was circulated in it. The first forest they came to was still living. Much of the trees that were hidden did not have as many leaves as the trees on the perimeter.

There was a skinny guard, with a silver chain, standing at the boundary. He was flinging the link around, as the company approached to talk. "Find your own forest. You are not welcome here."

"We know you have no hope in there," responded Alphason. "The outer trees cannot mask the truth of what's inside. We come from the New Word to compel you to listen to reason. Are you the dominant one here?"

"You may not come in. I'll bring the one you seek to you."

"We'll do as you wish." It didn't take long for a short chubby one to come out, accompanied by another. The follower he brought with him was the one a long time ago that was pulled from the river. He had blue eyes, but looked hollow inside.

"Let me guess," said the annoyed fat one, as he pulled out a piece of straw from his mouth he was sucking on. "You want us to join with the New Word again?"

"He is willing to forget the past to offer a way for you to survive. The New Word believes that his forest will last longer because the Tree of Knowledge is there. The Old Word destroyed the Tree of Life because he still has the other tree. This is his reasoning."

"You have got to be wordless. We will never follow that fool again. He told us the Tree of Life would be ours, and his kingdom will last forever. Now look at it. We will now suffer in ruins. Plus our river is fuller than his. Why would we go to your forest whose river has already dried up? Your Word continues to be a fool. We believe it is time for a New-*er* Word. One that has wisdom." Alphason found laughter he had not experienced in a while.

"What is so funny?" The fat one suddenly remembered something. "Wait, I know you. You're that man who the New Word tricked into following him. Why do you of all people continue to be with him?" Alphason had nothing to say, as he looked down to the ground. He forgot what it was that was so funny to him.

"I see. You are his slave. We are not. A long time ago, all of us were slaves to the Old Word, but not anymore."

"What are you now?"

"We are free now. We chose to follow the New Word at first, but not anymore. We follow ourselves." Alphason remembered the joke, as his laughter continued again.

"Only to wind up here to suffer in a world, without any nourishment. You are not free. The Old Word gave you real freedom to serve him, but now you are only slaves to yourselves. I see that now."

Alphason felt like he had just released a breath he had been holding ever since the fall. The hollow follower, who was standing by, found Alphason's words contagious. Giggling carried over to him. Life seemed to return to him, as he did not seem empty anymore. The dominant deserter looked at him with a stern look.

"How dare you mock me!"

"May I come with you?" asked the silent one to Alphason.

"You cannot go with him. You are not allowed."

"I thought you said you were free," confronted Alphason. "Why would you deny this one a choice?" The fat deserter thinks it over.

"Very well. But do not expect to come back here if you leave. We'll see whose laughing when that day comes."

**

As they continued their walk down the river to the Tree of Life, the new devotee followed. He ran up to Alphason, who was leading the group, to speak to him. "I want to thank you for including me in your group. But why are you headed this way? I thought your forest was behind us."

"It is, but our main purpose for our trip was to go back to the Tree of Life."

"What could you possibly hope to see from that place?"

"I don't know, but it has been a long time since any of us have been there. We need to find something that can get this garden to start growing again, and the answer must come from there."

"I see. Use me any way you see fit. I can be very helpful."

"Walk a little closer to me. I have something to tell you I don't want the others to hear." He did just that. "You want to have freedom?"

"I do." Alphason talked a little quieter.

"Then I suggest every time we venture out here you must tag along. Spend as much time away from the New Word as possible. He has no freedom for you."

"I deserted from him once. The only reason I am out here is because of you. You seem to carry more wisdom than anyone else around here. You are my Word."

"Even I can't give you freedom. The only one that can give you that is the Old Word. I believe that by serving him, there is hope."

"You know, I have no memory before I was pulled out of the river. I don't remember ever rebelling against the Old Word. There was fire in the sky. Before that, there was nothing."

"It may all come back to you. You were not the only one they found. Maybe the others can help you remember."

"They are still with the New Word. I rather stay out here with you."

"You've got the idea."

"What was that you said back there to the deserter?" shouted a searcher, who was following in the line behind him. There were no eyebrows on his face and his left hand was holding a grotesque-looking mask, resembling a serpent's head. "You don't still hold to the Old Word, do you?"

"I follow the one that has wisdom. Who do you think that is?" he said, as he looked behind him.

"The New Word, of course."

"We shall see."

**

When they arrived at the end of the river, which was shallow enough for a child to walk through, they found a leviathan that was near to death. It was lying in a moat of water covering a fraction of a

109

body that had starved itself. The moat surrounded a sandy mound in the center where the sword was stuck in the ground.

The metal seemed smaller than it was. There was a small flicker of flame left on it. Providing a way to cross the moat, the charred skeleton of the Tree of Life offered a bridge if they were willing to travel around to the other side.

"Is it safe to enter?" asked one of the followers, with a long yellow piece of cloth in his hand. His teeth were just as yellow.

"I wouldn't risk it, as long as that fire is still lit," warned Alphason. "However, the fire does seem to be burning out. When it does, then I think it will be safe, but not until then."

"But that may take another hundred years from now."

"Then so be it. At this point, news will be the only thing we will be able to take back with us."

"At least we will have something to look forward to. Maybe when the fire burns out, we can take the sword back with us. Wouldn't that be a wonderful treasure for our master?"

"We should probably head back. Let's make camp first and rest a little."

As they situated themselves along the side of the river, Alphason saw something near the edge of the water where the ground was still moist. He waited until the others had settled themselves before he would get a closer look.

As the last one had fallen asleep, he scaled down to it and found a plant, with a piece of stone fruit attached, that he could not identify. It was unusual for a variety such as this to not grow from a tree.

The ground he was at brought a memory back when he felt all hope was lost. It was the time when he thought the seed was gone forever. Five hundred years was but a moment in the span of eternity.

CHAPTER 24

The Hourglass

An account of the last days of the Tree of the Knowledge of Good and Evil.

When the searchers were ready to commence their journey at the setting sun, they were annoyed at the motionless body of Alphason, down by the river. He was prostrate out on the ground and his mouth was closed. "Why that lazy, spoiled brat!" grumbled the searcher, with the yellow cloth, as he went down and kicked him in the side. "Get up!"

The former deserter didn't like the violence displayed, as he rushed down himself. More life seemed to be returning to him and there was a time he could now remember when he felt compassion for another. Alphason was his paragon-of-past and it was his key to remembering. He felt a fierce sense of loyalty to him and wanted to kill the searcher that wouldn't stop the beating.

When he reached the ignorant follower, he grabbed hold of his yellow cloth that was dangling from his left hand. It was enough to get his attention, as he concluded his walloping and began to tug his paragon back. Noel wouldn't let go. "Unhand my treasure! Find your own gold."

"If you weren't such a fool you would have noticed that this man can no longer be hurt."

"What do you mean?"

"Look at him." Noel finally released the searcher's cloth, as his sympathetic anger turned to grief. "At least you still have your treasure. I fear the worst has happened to mine. He is no longer breathing."

"You mean to tell me that he is dead?"

"The Old Word will take it from here. The dust is where he'll return."

"Our master is not going to like this." The searchers moved on, but they were unaware of the weird plant next to him, missing its fruit.

**

Back at the forest of the Tree of the Knowledge of Good and Evil, two followers, both with half of a root in their hand, were standing over a lifeless body. It is lying in the middle of the crop of beans that had recently grown. "What are we to tell the New Word?"

"The truth," responded the other, whose voice had a similar soothing angelic voice. "He'll have to find a new gardener that could somehow replace her."

"I guess it will be meat every day ..." As they walked away, the hand that belonged to Evere seemed to have dropped an unknown piece of stone fruit. A bite was taken out of it. It had been picked from an unusual plant that seemed out of place in a ground meant for beans.

**

"Why does the Old Word take and take?!" cried the New Word as he paced himself in front of the Tree of Knowledge. Two halves of a root was in his hand. "At least I still have this tree, but it does not show me everything."

A follower approached him, whose hands appeared to be free of a paragon-of-past, but it was something he never took out for others to see. A diamond was what some believed he carried with him. "Sir, the searchers had returned."

"Hopefully they have something that can cheer me up."

"Alphason does not seem to be with them."

"Why did they leave him? Bring them to me immediately!" The searchers were brought over, as the New Word noticed the new one to the group. "Who is this?"

"We were able to compel at least one to come back with us," shared the one with the yellow cloth.

"You're the one we pulled out of the river. You made a wise choice. These are troubling times we are going through, however. Where is Alphason?"

"We are sorry to bring terrible news back with us, but Alphason has breathed his last."

"Both of them at the same time?"

"What do you mean, my Word?"

"It seems Evere is lost forever, as well."

"The Old Word must be up to something. We did find one thing that may provide hope that we discovered at the Tree of--"

"Death! It is now known as the Tree of Death."

"That is wise of you to say. The sword is still there, and its fire is burning out. It may be another century before it dies, but when it does the ground will be safe to enter and the sword will be yours." The Werd's mood was improved by this.

"This is good news. When the rest of the deserters see that we have this metal of the Old Word, surely they will beg to be on my side again. We will wait for this day to arrive."

**

A century was ruthless to the land, as the desert had fully taken over. The rest of the forests had since been completely covered over by the sand. One oasis remained, with enough life to allow the Tree of Knowledge to stand. Some deserters returned, but others were lost to the wasteland. They could not die, but they were condemned to suffer.

Searchers returned to the Tree of Life for the sword that had lost its flame. The moat surrounding it was filled with sand and offered no more life to the skeleton of the leviathan that had decomposed many years ago. Other skeletons littered the world from what was left of the giant beasts.

They succeeded in entering the center, as they stood over the rusting metal that was now the size for a fully grown man to carry. "The Tree of Death is no longer protected by the Old Word. I believe he will no longer have any use for this."

The searcher laid his cloth on top of it, as he breathed a sigh of relief when nothing happened to him. With a couple of yanks, the sword was released from its centuries-long cradle, as sand poured down the hole it was stuck in.

The searchers walked away and were unaware of what was going on behind them. The sand did not cease to fall, and the mound began to sink.

**

The searchers returned to the oasis and desired to present their prized possession to the New Word. The day had come, but the New Word was covered with extra robes, for he could not hide. The oasis was green without any trees, except for the Tree of Knowledge. "Master, the wait is over."

"You have brought me great pleasure in a time of suffering," replied the Werd.

The follower, with the spyglass was peering across the great desert. "I see deserters in the distance."

"Have they finally found us?"

"I can't explain it, but for some reason they seem to be sinking in the sand out there."

"I don't understand. How would they be sinking? There is no water out there." He looks to the searchers holding the sword. An unnerving thought struck him. "You fools!

Put it back!"

"You told us to bring it to you." The Werd's hand was poking through the robes, with a diamond in his hand, pointing at the sword.

"I had no reasoning to go off of that I would know it would cause this. This tree shows me only what it wants to show me."

"What are we to do?"

"We stay close to the tree. I still don't believe he will destroy it."

**

Back at ground zero, a giant crater had replaced what used to be a mound. The sand continued to fall into an increasingly widening hole. When the crater became deep enough, skeletons of whales were uncovered. It was almost as if they came back to life, for they appeared to be swimming. The sand underneath was what was pushing them, as the whirlpool began to form.

**

The night had fallen, and the stars above the oasis seemed to be in motion. "What are we to think of this?" noticed one of the followers, who was pointing to the sky with a dagger. It had a special word inscribed on it. "Even the stars seem affected by our apocalypse."

"The stars are not what's moving," said the New Word, as he looked upon waves of sand in the desert. The others saw it too.

"It looks like an ocean. Is it the sand that moves?"

"We are the ones that are moving to wherever the Old Word takes us. I want you all to grab on to the Tree of the Knowledge of Good and Evil and never let go. Wherever he sends us will be to wherever the roots of the tree will lead."

This became challenging, as the forces around them became stronger, casting off the weaker ones. The Werd tied a yellow cloth he had around the tree and his waist, so he would not fall off. The patch of grass they were on was like a raft, as it was tossed around in a cyclone of sand. Eventually, the centrifugal force kept the ones who were strong enough from falling off. The whole world could not escape the vortex, as everything was sucked down into a black hole, with unknown origins.

Darkness was found on the other side, as the sand began to rise. Fear had carried up to this place. It is the link between the Word and the wordless. A new kind of fear was added to the knowledge of deteriorating souls, who chose an unfortunate fate. As a keeper of the things to come, the hourglass formed the boundaries of a new-er age.

Peace and joy reigned in the world long before this fear reached its end. The hourglass becomes a mirror into this future. The sand becomes a snowrise, along a fresh landscape. An ancient evil has lifted its fear to this place where there is no tree to hide in front. Those who hope for a better world will find it over ice and fire.

Rest had found the helper, as she lay underneath a frozen bed. A slow, shallow breathing proved that there was still life within her, as the peace turned into a struggle. She lurched down and exhaled a deep breath.

Evere was alone in a topsy-turvy world that looked much like the desert she was used to, but this place was cold and white. She had to shake her head and squint to bring her world to her viewpoint. The sky and ground was back the way she remembered it.

The brown coat she had on was not enough, as a chill found her. It was a temperature she had never felt before. A second layer of coat was discovered close to her. It shared the same color as the soft ground she sat upon and seemed very heavy and furry.

She thanked the Word, as she slipped it on and rose up. It was a better world she sensed that was ahead of her, but one that was in need of progress. Hope led the way, as she set out on her journey to discover the good unclaimed!

PART IV
THE BELL

CHAPTER 25

In the Valley of the Shadow of Death

The New Word had a name a long time ago that was given to him by the Old Word. He was referred to only as the W. It was a time when one served the other. The creatures that walked the earth, swam in the sea and called sky their home all had only one master.

There was a special word that the Old Word would use, and it would bring the animal kind under his care. Things changed when the W learned of this word. The rebellion was born within him. He was able to convince others to join with him and thus changing his name to the We.

They were all cast out of heaven into a pasture of sheep, and it became time for the We to use the word he had knowledge of to take what he believed was his share of the creation. He disguised himself as a wolf and named himself the Wer[8]. The word was uttered as some, but not all went under the authority of the Wer.

He became furious that the word was not strong enough to change all of them because the Old Word had used a new word. It would forever be a mystery to those who are ashamed. Only those that the Old Word called his own would know of this word. When the word was uttered, those that belonged to the Old Word would hear it. For those who hated him, a bell would ring, causing the wicked to never hear the call. Being

---

[8]   Wer (wâr)

cut off from this knowledge, the Wer desired to know this new word and would later change his name to the Werd.

**

Ghost found bells helpful in his misadventures. Whenever he met with a test that was too challenging, a bell would ring. Not to confuse him, because the mighty dog was one of those who could hear the call of the Old Word.

There is one bell in particular that is yet to be rung, as Ghost sprints across the world towards a showdown between good and evil. The journeyman thinks it would be useful if he could ride on his back, as he believes this would be more effective to find the helper quicker. There is nothing to hold on to, and Alphason refuses to ride inside the dog's mouth again. No matter how many times he falls off, he still believes it would cover more ground faster this way.

A wide chasm over a very deep valley brings their journey to a standstill. Alphason dismounts clumsily off the dog and walks to the edge, as he looks down. He detects no bottom to it. "How are we going to cross over?" He looks to the right and left but sees no end to the valley. "There's no way you can jump this. How did you get all the way up that mountain? If you can accomplish that, then this can't be too small a task for something as great as you."

The dog kneels to help the man get back on top. "You have a plan, don't you?" When he sits, the giant begins backing up. "Jumping is your idea? This is unwise."

As the dash begins, the rider tries to hang on to the fur and recognizes falling off this time would be the end for him. Right before the man starts to fall off, the dog launches himself over. It is a commendable leap, but he begins declining too early. The dog uses what muscle he could, as he bumps the man who is hanging by the feathery tail to sail him the rest of the way. It succeeds, as Alphason crashes on the other side, but the giant continues to fall into the darkness below. The journeyman rushes to the edge, as he hopes the dog found some kind of ledge. There is no sign of life. It looks like death below.

He is surprised to feel emotion for the poor beast. He's been separated from him before, but this feels different. "I just don't believe that this is it for him. His story can't end here." After a long moment passes, Alphason decides to concede to a harsher reality and continue his journey alone. It is a sadder road ahead for him.

As he walks away, a soft ringing is heard behind him, as he turns his head. There is nothing there, but by his side walks the ghost, as if nothing happened. Alphason cannot find the words he feels from this confusing surprise. "Okay, what's your secret? I would love to know what you know. Let's walk a little before I try to get back on top of you. I'm aching a little bit from the bumpy ride."

In the valley of the shadow of death, a sliver of light from the top cannot reach the bottom. Another light is provided by a torch, carried by a gangly member of the fallen sand, with a gold ring on his finger. He would rather be anywhere else but down here. "Master, where are you? The others said you would be here."

He can barely walk, with his trembling legs and manages to trip over his own feet. The torch is dropped, as it rolls down a rock and stops just short of an empty nest that belongs to another giant. "This is insanity! Why would he come to a place like this?!" He gets up, grabs the torch and decides not to stay any longer as he runs.

"Stay where you are!" yells the Werd from somewhere in the darkness. The follower obeys.

"My Werd, there is danger here. Why do you come? Is it not enough that those birds have diminished our numbers greatly that you locate their lair?" The trembling legs cannot hold him up any longer, as he sinks to the ground. He refuses to release the torch again from his hand, as the Werd finally reveals himself walking towards his light. A dagger is in his hand. "I am ashamed of my cries."

"Your fear is being held in my hand." The Werd kneels down to his hunkered level and touches his shoulder providing comfort. "I have much use for cowards like yourself. You will fit greatly in my world. This same fear you now possess will keep this world under our submission. The fear is not intended for the ones that are closest to me."

"But why are you here?"

"Fear will be needed to bring an end to those dreadful birds. They may not be afraid of us, but they will soon learn to be." The Werd studies the torch in his hand. "I see you have found some wood. Has the divination been fulfilled?"

"Just like you said. There is more wood than you can possibly imagine now. The others have been readying a great fire in our hall. We would like you to come see it."

"This would please me greatly." The follower still seems to be troubled. "What brings you suffering still?"

"Many of us have volunteered to retrieve this wood, but many of us have not come back."

"The time has now come for the word that I uttered to the sheep and the beasts of the garden that brought them under my control to be used again. This is a lair we are now in, but it does not belong to the ones that hunt us. I suggest you stay low to the ground where you are. There are many of them." The Werd stands back up and faces the darkness, as he holds out his dagger. "Cover your ears, coward. It is not your place to hear this." The follower obeys.

As the word is uttered, a great rustling cannot be muted by the cowering follower. He continues to keep his ears covered but spies a flood of black feathers, spilling out of the top of the valley.

After the last one leaves, he remembers there is something else he is supposed to tell the Werd. "Is it okay to release my ears, master?" The Werd turns around and nods his head. "There was one other thing I was supposed to tell you, but what were those things I saw?"

"Those white birds will no longer be a threat to us. They will be greatly mismatched against the crow. What else did you have to say?"

"You are not going to like this. On our wanderings outside to find the wood, we have discovered that both are still alive."

"Evere *and* Alphason?"

"I have brought you grief." The Werd loses control, as he storms toward the follower. He stops just short of his face, shouting at him.

"You mean to tell me that after everything they have done, the Old Word still cares for those ungrateful mortals?!!"

"Have you lost?"

"No, I have not lost! If I can't have them. Then neither one of us will have them. They are still going to die. The Old Word gave them life; then I will bring them death." He turns back to the darkness one more time. "While my crow will be busy with the white menace, my vulture and raven will have their moment in history."

CHAPTER 26

Unknown, but not Forgotten

Somebody else inhabits the darkness. It is a place he has grown accustomed to, for he is someone who is unknown to many. It was a trick of his to get lost in the crowd and never get noticed by the New Word. He preferred to stay out of the way of most of what was going on.

He heard the conversation that took place in the lair of the crow. The follower, with the ring on his finger, led him here unaware. There were whisperings of another conspiracy he thought to tell them about but he is now growing disillusioned of his own loyalties. He begins to wonder if he should follow a different path.

This fire that is being readied was something he preferred to stay away from, so he chose not to bring a torch with him. The tunnel he trailed the follower down will lead him back to the hall where the rest of the fallen sand are, but another tunnel was discovered when he entered the dark valley. There is no foreseeing where it could lead.

Without the fire, it would be complete darkness going down it. This decision would not be made lightly. He will have to trust his sense of touch to find his way through. It is a good thing he had no paragon-of-past, so he could use both of his hands to make it work.

A decision is made when the follower, with the ring, begins running down the tunnel towards the fire. He is too quick to catch up to, so it would be darkness either way. Something inside him senses that disaster awaited this gangly one.

The New Word is still in the lair of the crow. He could hear his heavy breathing. It conjures a fear that motivates him to feel his way down the unexplored tunnel. "I thought I sensed someone else in here."

He had never felt this kind of anxiety when the New Word spoke. The thought of deserting brings out this feeling like never before. "Where do you think you're going?"

The voice sounds closer. It has to mean that he is being followed. He hoped that he didn't have to hurry his way through the tunnel in fear of falling down a hole, or gashing his knee on a rock. It seems like no easy choice is left. "Why do you remain silent? I know you're there."

He runs with his hands out forward, hoping he can at least protect his head. A hole is discovered and it was something he almost fell into if it wasn't for his hands being free to brace himself. The next problem is trying to find a way around a pit he isn't sure how wide it could be. For all he knows, it could be an abyss. "I have grown wearisome of deserters. No more will I allow dissent. I will feed you to the fire. The crow will take you there."

The voice is growing louder, and there is no time to study the drop. With the little room he has left, he begins backing up to a point to where he could feel the Werd breathing down his neck. "Can you smell the burning yet?"

He remembers something when the Werd grabs his arm. The deceiver is not someone of great physical strength. It is the words he uses that keeps his fallen sand trapped. His fear escapes him when he considers this. "I can smell the flesh the fire will eat and now I have it in my hand."

The tunnel holds no more fear for him too, as he easily breaks the grip of the Werd and races towards the pit. His jump breaks through his cowardly ways but realizes he may have been slightly foolish, due to a hole that has no other side to it. Thankfully, the bottom isn't as far as he thought it was as he falls to a ground that at least gives him a few scrapes. "Another deserter bites the dust, I see. This hole should take care of that."

He could hear him at the top, and there is no way he is going to let it be known how shallow the pit is. "If you can still hear me down there.

I would suggest that you stay where you are. Don't you even think about going outside where the crow are warring."

Outside is exactly the place he desires to be. There is no way he is going to let the Werd's fear get to him again. No more words are uttered from the dark one who seems to have left for those still under his spell.

He notices that the rocky ground he is on has a slight incline in it. It also feels a little cooler, due to a slight draft that reaches his cuts. His legs are still functioning, as he stands up and begins the climb up the hill.

It may have seemed like a long ramp, but the farther he travels, the colder he feels. He knows the direction he is going is certain, and he longs to see the stars again. Exposure to his enemies may be a risk, but it comes with great reward that he is already feeling.

A glint of light can be seen at the top. He knows it has to be dark outside, but it is brighter than it is in here. There are lights that were created that governed the night, as well.

A voice can be heard again, but it is within him like a still water. A shepherd is speaking to him. It causes his want to subside and makes his desire to be with the Word that created him.

A path of righteousness is set before him. Even though he has walked through the shadow of death, there was never any real fear of evil. Someday there will be green pastures to lie in.

The tunnel he is in is much wider he discovers when he gets closer to the top. More light is pouring into the cavern. There is what looks like a crow ahead of him, walking its own path towards the exit. It is unaware of what is behind it because it is only interested in what is ahead. A grand arching exit between the cave and the rest of the world provides room for this giant to come and go. It is like a curtain in an opera house opening up, as the stars unveil the closer they approach.

As the crow flies off, it is a table in the sky that is set before him in the presence of his enemies. Other crows are seen gliding across it but are unaware of the rod and staff that comforts him. Forever there will be dwelling in the house of the Lord. Surely goodness and mercy will follow his days. The Word will guide him there.

CHAPTER 27

The Massacre

The crow is a very intelligent species. It is one of the smartest in the animal kingdom. The white bird is precious to the Old Word. It is a creation of his that was made with great delicacy and wonder. They are unprepared for a threat of this kind. Not many would invite a war with the superior crow.

Ghost and Alphason had already traveled a half a mile past the valley of shadow. It has become a slower walk for the two travelers. They are growing weary at the journey that has proven longer than they were hoping.

It is quiet between them, as attempts to converse from the man becomes more stagnant. They prefer to use the energy they have left to walk instead of talk. The silence between them makes it possible to hear a slight noise behind them. They turn around to observe what looks like a black storm is coming their way. They both fall to the ground as they try to blend in with the snow around them. The storm passes over the two ghosts, and it seems whatever is in it is uninterested in them.

**

The storm coordinates to space themselves out to provide more silence that would give them a stealth advantage. When the first white wing is located, the entire storm keeps at a distance but is zeroed in to see where it would lead them. The bird of wonder is hunting, as well. It locates a follower on the ground, as it grabs him without any trouble.

Eventually, the first wonder leads them to another white bird, who seems to be flying with a similar destination. The two unknowingly succeed in leading the silent storm to a numerous multitude of white wings all with the same flight plan.

They reach a point in the sky where the white birds seem to be flying in circles. It looks to be a home in the sky for them. They are all gliding down to a ground that is surrounded by a mountain range that shows no way out unless those who find themselves there have a pair wings.

The first white bird drops the follower from its talons, before it lands itself in the circle. It is a place of rest for the birds and offers no chance of escape for the prey that are brought here. The follower is among other fallen sand who are frantically searching for a way out. They all are aware of what would happen to them if they linger here for too long.

When the last white bird grounds, the storm reaches the arena as they perch themselves on top of the rocky walls. They wait for their moment until the very last one is asleep.

Peace passes over the multitude as a black bird that seems more menacing than the others flies down to the very center. He is scarred by inner feuds from his own kind, making him the alpha male. It is his place to lead his executioners into their first battle and take great risks; such as this one in the midst of hostile sleepers.

He manages to not startle any of them, then proceeds to squawk loud enough to wake the entire flock. They wake and see the one that seems outnumbered, as the white birds closest to him begin advancing. They are not the ones with the upper hand, as the rest who are perched on top of the mountain swarm in an ambush.

The massacre begins without much loss to the crow. For the white bird, however, the cost is great. After the last one is slaughtered, the crow leave the grave-like battleground, along with the trapped fallen sand.

The abandoned followers beg to be rescued, but the crows only have one mission to accomplish. There are other white birds in the sky who are isolated and are easy to track down. The crow recognize they will all eventually lead to the fiery mountain. When they are found, they are executed without trouble and quickly become endangered. They are soon to become extinct; never to be seen again or whispered of throughout the annals of time.

The last one is still out there.

CHAPTER 28

Stories

The last of the birds of wonder is not a strong one. It is still broken and incapable of flight and is still under the care of Evere. The stories she has been telling it seems to have brought him under a sleep. This is a good thing for she had run out of history to share. She looks up to the sky that has more stars than she had ever counted before. "You're going to think I'm crazy, but I believe all of the stars up there has a story to tell. One story for each of them. I would love to go there someday to know their secrets. The moon beams brighter than all of them because its story is the greatest of them all."

She is confused as to why this particular night the moon did not appear. "Where did it go? It must be hiding." The moment she looks back down, a full moon unveils. Behind her in the snow, a silent killer keeps its distance. It is the raven that stands in her shadow.

**

Nearing the end of a long journey, Alphason has confidence that Ghost knows where he is going and believes they are getting closer to the helper. Snow still covers the whole ground, but it feels a tad warmer. More trees had surfaced, bringing their world into the present.

One particular tree catches their fascination that appears over the horizon. Alphason begins commenting on what he sees when they get closer to identify its features. "If it is a tree, it's the ugliest looking sprout I've ever seen."

It got to a point to where feathers could be viewed on it. "I don't think it is a tree." What they discover is an aberrant giant of a bird whose only color on its body is pitch black. It has a long slender neck, drooping down its front with its eyes closed. "It's either dead or just sleeping."

They pass by it without trouble, as they continue onward. "The Old Word should give this lazy one something to do. He stays there long enough a tree might sprout underneath him." Alphason laughs at his mocking and turns his head back towards it. He is slightly disturbed at what he sees. "I believe that laughter has its time and place. This is not one of them." The vulture is still frozen and lifeless, but is now turned towards them. His eyes are still closed, but it feels like darkness is peering into their souls.

**

The kind of dreams a bird of wonder has is a nice thought to ponder. Who can fathom such a mind? It wakes up to a nightmare when it opens its eyes. It becomes greatly agitated and releases a deafening squawk. "What is the matter with you?"

Evere turns to face her assassin that has its giant crooked legs reaching out to grab her. She lets out a blistering scream that almost covers up a thunderous clanging from a distant hammer. The ground underneath the woman and the white bird erupts from the snow into a tall pillar. The inertia from the sudden movement keeps the two ascending upwards, even though the pillar has reached its climax. Gravity finally takes effect, bringing Evere back down with minor bruises. The white bird remains in the air a little longer, as it tries to flap its broken wings, eventually leading back to where Evere is.

The timely structure manages to bring them out of danger, but as Evere peers back down to the ground where the raven is she sees their safety is going to be brief. Birds do have the ability to fly.

Evere looks to the other side and sees something else flying over the cliff she had stood on before she befriended the white bird. It seems like it is a setup. The ground they are on is a trap because another threat has entered the area. A single crow sent to kill off the rest of the white wings is flying over the cliff. Death and persecution seems to be in store for them with nowhere to run.

**

Every time Ghost and Alphason look at the aberrant it seems to have repositioned itself as if it is following them. The dog loses enough of its comfort to decide that it is a real threat, as he stands in front of the journeyman, growling at the vulture.

Alphason couldn't see around the dog as he moves to the left to get a better look. The vulture is gone as he gazes up towards the big head of Ghost who is not looking in the same direction that he is looking in. The dog's covered eyes are facing behind him where the vulture now plants itself. It is standing frozen a tree's length away from him.

The man decides it is time to run, as the vulture's long neck begins slowly lurching upwards. The eyes are now open, as it looks towards the fleeing journeyman. It lets out an extended mournful squawk. Alphason's legs buckle for some reason, as he falls face forward on the ground. He feels the darkness within him as his body quits, making it impossible for him to get back up. It is like being paralyzed. The vulture, however, has full use of its functions, as it hobbles over.

**

Death from below almost reaches the top, as persecution is setting up for an attack from the sky. Clanging thunder is heard over the land again, as another pillar erupts from the ground. It is close enough to jump to, but Evere hesitates as she wonders how the bird of wonder is going to make it. "I'm sorry," is all she can say, as she leaps to the second pillar.

Thunder continues as a third pillar followed by others shoot up providing a leaping path away from danger. When she reaches the fifth pillar, the sixth looks to be too far away. She should have waited, as another pillar comes up from the ground, providing an easier leap. She had already committed to the impossible and she is now falling towards a ground that would kill a giant.

**

It would have been an easy neck to get to for the dog. Many beasts have become victims to his terrible teeth. Birds, however, are still his weakness. Every time Ghost would get close enough to attack, the darkness uses its wings to hop over to the paralyzed prey.

The dog runs over to the journeyman as he figures if he can't kill the vulture than he can still protect his friend. The mournful squawk of the aberrant is released again. This time it causes the dog to fall over, nearly landing on Alphason. There is no more resistance for the vulture, as it hops towards where there are now two paralyzed on the ground.

**

Evere closes her eyes, as she did not want to witness the long-awaited end to her life. When she opens them again, it is not death she finds or the dust she would someday return to, but a snow-tipped pillar and the sight of a broken white bird who has somehow caught up with her on the next one. She leaps over to it, but it now looks more broken than it was before. "I thought I was falling to the end of my life. Only you could have saved me."

She does not see death or persecution anywhere in the sky, coming after them. There are more pillars to jump to. "I wish I could help you. I have not the ability to revive you. The Old Word will have to take it from here. Thank you for honoring me with your precious life. Remember my stories," is the last thing she says as she jumps to the next platform.

There is an end to the pillars. A grand mountain range is ascending in the distance that Evere is certain the trail in the sky is leading to.

**

Ghost wonders if the bells are too busy to come to his rescue this time. Darkness is now looming over them, as it stretches down its neck to peck at the journeyman's lifeless limbs.

The dog is too much of a believer to allow the darkness to reach his head, as he still has use of what is above the neck. He looks to the left and right to see if a plan is within view. Nothing is provided, but an idea does start to form. A long time ago the Old Word gave him everything he needed to be a protector. Teeth to tear into annoying beasts, legs that can almost keep up with the wind, a coat that can change its color and a long tongue that can be useful for a moment like this.

The first peck from the darkness scars the prey's arm. Before he could tear into him again, the journeyman finds himself inside the mouth of the big head lying beside him. The squawk that comes from the vulture's mouth is no longer mournful, but is agitated for it cannot get to the man he is sent for. He proceeds to pick at the fur of Ghost to get him to release his friend. The dog remains stubborn, as his body is presented as a replacement for the journeyman's suffering.

**

A black cloud, with lightning brewing is setting over the mountain. The crag offered a path where Evere had collapsed, as she tries to regain her strength. Even though it is a dark cloud above, wondrous light is all that she marveled at, flickering in its vapor. She has no prior knowledge of this and the rain that she feels on her face.

It becomes too warm for her, as she takes the white second layer off and finds the first brown one is enough. When she regains enough strength to carry on, she follows the path she is on. It leads her to a dense forest that is within the walls of the mountain. Optimism follows her in here. She feels like she has entered a new world. It is a place that she could get lost in.

She is not ready for the first lightning that hit a tree close by. The noise from the thunder was so great, she is certain she is deaf. The optimism escapes her, and when she looks over at the path, she was previously on, persecution is seen scaling down it. Life force is on its beak. Full extinction of the white bird had been achieved.

Evere uses her hand to hold back an anguished sympathetic cry. There is an attempt to find reason in all of this, as she tries to calm down. She hopes that the Old Word has a resting place for it. Maybe not here, but maybe somewhere that the bird had dreamed of in its sleep.

It may have all been wishful thinking, but she believes the Old Word didn't bring her this far to take her away from hope.

The crow has not become aware of Evere just yet as she is covered in the crowded trees. The forest is also very dark, as she feels her way to another side where persecution cannot follow her. Just enough light is being provided by the flash of the lightning, followed by ear-shattering thunder.

By the second or third strike, Evere's ears really had become shattered and relies only on her sight and touch to find safety. Heavy rain effects these senses as well. She is able to make out a falling tree, crashing into a rocky wall that was struck by lightning. It shows a possible way out of this place. Evere fears the longer she stays lost here, the giant crow will eventually discover her.

When she reaches the tree, she sees the top is leaning on a ledge. The log is somewhat shaky but is wide enough to keep her from falling off. Fatigue sets in when she reaches the top, as she sits to catch her breath.

She uses this time to think about things and wonders if there is anything left to fear. Maybe there is nothing to worry about if she is to die. If the Old Word will take care of the bird of wonder, then maybe he'll take care of her. She has no proof to go on about the afterlife other than the path the Old Word seems to be providing for her now, but she seems to be led into one trap after another. Maybe it is her guilt that persecutes her, leading her to more dangers despite the Old Word's efforts.

In fact, persecution is currently heading up the fallen tree she was just on. This startles her out of her thoughts, as she frantically looks for her next escape. She sees that the ledge she is on has more going on than she first realized. It leads up towards a cave. The crow still does not seem to notice her, as she walks quietly up the path.

When she reaches the cave, it does not offer a less intimidating atmosphere. The end of this place is uncertain. Even though she couldn't see, she decides to pretend that the darkness is far away from her, as she looks to the lightning flashes that guides her senses. She enters but still brings her fear in with her that her imagination cannot hide.

Her imagination makes her see things that aren't there in the black. One thing she cannot unsee is a glare from what looks like the end of the cave. The lightning reveals death in its hiding place. It did not seem to see her, as she holds her hand over her mouth to prevent a scream. She runs back out and halfway down the path, but sure enough persecution is at the bottom walking up towards her. It is another trap for her fear.

The cave is now vacant, as the raven now stands outside its entrance. Neither one has noticed her. If she is to jump from this ledge, it might be a less painful end but it certainly will kill her.

She looks up to the lights in the sky from the dark cloud and refuses to look at death and persecution, coming for her. The light holds hope for her. Lightning reveals that the top of the mountain is not much farther away. Enough rocks are protruding from the wall to be used as steps, which could provide a possible steep way out.

It is enough of a prompting to attempt it, as she reaches her hand out for the first step. The first couple of steps are easy enough, but it feels like the river again when she makes it halfway. It is the same distance either away, but no matter what her body feels, her mind is determined to keep her arms and legs moving. She sees each lightning strike as strength being given to her.

If she is to look down, she would see the crow and raven who have found each other and are engaged in a bird fight. She is too deaf to hear them.

There is no energy left in her when she reaches the top, except for what is needed to get her legs up to the surface where the rest of her body is. She is almost hit by the lightning this time, as one strikes with the brightest blue in its charge over the cliff she just climbed off of.

When an ounce of strength comes back to her, she rolls over and looks down to two lifeless bodies, belonging to two black birds at the bottom. Smoke is lifting off of the feathers. It is a good place for her to rest for a while, as she invites sleep to her debilitated body. Her dreams are where Alphason lives.

**

Ghost had endured hours of torture from the vulture that relentlessly picked at him with its gnarly beak. He will not allow the darkness to reach the one he was appointed to protect again. Much life force was shed, but the darkness cannot completely cover up the fur.

The dog's color can no longer be considered white anymore, it is blending in with the light that comes from the brightest star appearing in the heaven above them. Blue, pink, orange and many other colors are in its mix. It is a soft light, but it is too much for the darkness, as it gives up and flies away.

When Ghost becomes convinced the vulture would not come back, he releases the man back to the snow. The darkness had left, as Alphason finds life back in his body. The light continues to surface off of the dog, keeping the danger away, but it is the crimson stained in the light that the journeyman saw. It is enough to bring a grown man to tears, as he looks upon his protector that is too weakened to stand at his side again. Ghost's journey has reached his end.

If it was not the greatest story of them all, then the Word itself will provide a suitable end, but be forewarned – it has no end.

CHAPTER 29

In the Chamber of the Life of Light

The light that arose from the dog's body was not his light. It was patterned off of a star that appeared in the sky. The light, however, did not originate from the star but was illuminated by a series of events, involving a room that was a secret until the New Word and his fallen sand discovered it.

The room they were previously in they had built a great fire that proved to be too hot for the miserable underground dwellers. A new tunnel was discovered that led them to a different chamber that was the biggest one yet.

They could not go back because the fire in the previous room had become too out of control and blocked the tunnel. Torches were brought over to help them explore the room. The fire created a reaction in a painting on the wall that grew in its source and spread throughout the chamber. It showed a vast story chronicled that must have led until the end of time, but the top was where it ended.

From the top in the center of the room, a silver bell hung with colossal dimensions. Abnormally-sized hammerhead bats were perched on it. The New Word brought his dagger out once again to speak the word that would bring reverence to these creatures.

The moment after he got the word out, what was believed first to be an earthquake was felt in the stone walls around them, but it was closer to something or someone was banging on the rock from the outside. The bell slowly began to swing, causing the gong on the inside to bang against the metal. Loud ringing drowned out the word used by the Old Word so the nefarious could not hear it.

This great power was strong enough to bring the ground underneath the sand to collapse underneath them into a bottomless pit. The foundationless fell downwards. At the same moment, the top of the ceiling was collapsing down the pit as well, and a face of a giant man was staring down from it. His eyes were smiling and his mouth was open as a tempest blew throughout the cavern.

The Werd managed to use the power of the word he had knowledge of to bring the bats under his control. The cave inhabitants obeyed his call, as they flew down and grabbed as many of the fallen as there were bats. It was too late for the Werd, however, as there was no bat for him.

A colorful light from a bottom with no beginning was purging through the hole, hitting the bell. Whose purity was so great, it reflected the light to the top of the open ceiling into a sky with no end. The light continued where the cave painting ended. There were other bells amongst the stars that continued reflecting the light across an endless universe that could provide room for its life.

The star that was patterned by the ghost was not a star.

CHAPTER 30

A Point of No Return

Alphason is burying himself in the soft glow of the fur and does not care for the life force that smears onto him. He is listening to a breathing that becomes more and more shallow. If this is to be his last moment with his protector, he is still going to need help to keep away the darkness.

A handful of fur is in his hand that was shed off of the beast. The light is rationed into his palm and would be useful in keeping aberrant birds away. "Thank you for this." He lets his tears wash away the life force that has not yet permanently stained in the fur. His other hand is on the dog's belly, as he feels the last breath release from him and his covered eyes close.

**

The whistle that comes next is not for Alphason. It reaches the ears of Ghost, however, as his newly trimmed eyes open back up once again and proceeds to stand. Health seems to have returned to him, but Alphason doesn't seem to notice. He looks to be woeful still. Ghost barks at him, but for some reason the journeyman does not hear it.

The ground he is standing on is different as the one Ghost is on. Snow is buried under the dog's feet, but grass is underneath Alphason. It is as if they are standing in different worlds. "I guess this is where we part," says the man with great difficulty.

Another whistling is heard by the dog, as the moment he's been waiting for has arrived. A season has come to an end, as he begins to walk into the winter away from Alphason. He looks behind one more time at the human, as he attempts one last bark towards his friend. The man is looking at the spring ahead of him and would never look to his ghost again.

The journeyman is confused about a grand rocky structure ahead of him. "Where did that mountain come from?" he asks himself. It is a name he chose to give for a phenomenon like this.

CHAPTER 31

A Long Marathon

The journeyman finally gives up the ghost, as he places the fur in his pocket where he found the seed a long time ago. It is much warmer here at the foot of the mountain, as he takes his white coat off and begins to explore this phenomenon. He locates a path that leads him into a dense forest. A light rain falls which is a pleasant new feeling for him. It is very dark inside the forest, as he takes out his fur again and uses it to provide enough light to find his way through.

A fallen tree is discovered, leaning against a cliff, as he climbs his way up. The ledge leads up to a cave. He walks halfway up the path and tries to avoid two giant black birds who appear to be dead. When the light from the fur hits them, they miraculously shrink to the size of Alphason's feet. "The darkness is brought into the light," he concludes.

A white fur coat is near the raven's crooked feet. He figures it must have found it before it died. A terrible thought occurs to him that Evere may have been a victim of this dreadful thing. Another thought surfaces with it that if she isn't dead then she must be near. "Evere! Do you hear me?"

**

Evere is lying on top of the mountain right above him but could not hear the shouts from below. The thunder may have had a lasting effect on her. She wakes from her dream and finds life again to move forward.

She stands up and begins walking towards the endless night ahead of her where other mountains offer future challenges in the distance. She is thankful it will be a while before she reaches them.

She cannot hear the flapping behind her where two hammerhead bats, carrying followers are dropped. One has the dagger in his hand. The other, with a ring on his finger, holds the rusting sword they pulled from the desert. They are shouting at her, but she could not hear, as she continues walking.

The one with the dagger flings his weapon at her but misses, as it stabs into the ground in front of her. This gets her attention, as she turns towards her agitators. "Are you deaf?! Do not take one more step until our sword has finished you."

"Why is it you that finds me? Where's Alphason?"

"Here!" They all look behind them and sees Alphason, who had just climbed on top to where they are. The fur that Alphason has is currently in his pocket that he had to put there in order to climb. He removes it, creating a resistance in the followers.

"Stay where you are!" The one with the sword runs behind Evere. "If you take one more step. You will never see her again. This time we mean it."

He puts the fur back in his pocket. "It's hidden," he says, as he begins advancing. "Where's the others at? What happened to the New Word?"

"What do you mean?" asks the other one who is bending down to retrieve the dagger. When he stands back up, an orange afro is now on his head that wasn't there before. "I'm right here."

"Why do you trouble us still? Why don't you let her go?"

"I have decided to kill you, but since our numbers have recently decreased significantly, I am willing to take you as slaves again." Alphason continues his advancement towards them.

"I think I get it now what it means to be a slave. At some point, the slave no longer can be himself but must be possessed by the master to where there is no more slave anymore. There is only him."

"What are you talking about?" probes the one holding the sword.

"You cannot see it, but it is something I have discovered from my many years of being in the desert. You believe he has the ability to do many wondrous things, like moving through thin air. Really it's him possessing each one of you and when he does you have no memory of it."

"Is this true?" he asks his master. "Yes, it is true," admits the New Word who is now the one holding the sword. "But he'll never figure it out." The one holding the dagger is bald now and is unaware of what just happened to him. When Alphason walks half the distance, the New Word and the follower become further unhinged. "Wait! I thought you were alone. Do not come any closer." Alphason looks around him and sees nothing.

"I do not scare others easily," he says, as he continues walking. "I am alone."

"This one is deaf and you are blind. I said stay right there!" He takes the sword right up to Evere's neck but drops it, as he and the follower begin backing off. Small footprints are leading towards them in the mud, but no one could be seen making them.

Laughter is heard from the child. The New Word drops the sword as him, and the follower waste no more time running towards the bats that are waiting in the sky. They are picked up and flown away to their loose ends that will forever lead them to chaos.

Alphason takes his remaining steps towards an Evere, who has just noticed the unusual footprints that are moving in circles around her. "What is it?" she asks.

"We've met before." Evere does not react, as if she hears his words. "They said you were deaf now." He studies her staring at the busy footprints that seem to be at play. "You are still beautiful to me. We will have to find a new way to communicate."

The footprints begin steering away from them and heads toward the mountains in the far distance. Evere and Alphason both begin running after it. They suppose that wherever they are to go, the child will lead them.

**

It is a long marathon. The child never tires. Exhaustion eventually catches up with the adults, causing them to give up. His footprints continue towards the mountains, as the trail becomes lost. Something else begins to tug at them. Rising above the mountains, a sun begins to climb. The first day in the new world has finally begun.

The child seems to take an interest in them. They believe that if they wait long enough, he would eventually want to play again. They choose to use the new day to relax and teach each other a new language they could use to communicate again. One not made up from sound, but of letters and words. It is going to take a while, with there being so many things to identify words for. 'Sun' is the first word they agree to.

This long drawn out task would lead to many days, exploring the world around them to find new things to create words for. Wherever they venture, they decide to keep the mountains within view in hopes of reuniting with the child again.

Most of the words are easy enough, but one particular day meets with a challenge. They have spent so much time waiting; summer passes, and fall arrives and it is time for Alphason to convert Evere into eating meat. She is sickened by the idea that Alphason had eaten the flesh of the bird. After he tells her the story about Ghost through the new written words, she begins to warm up to the idea.

The next hurdle is for Alphason to teach himself how to hunt. Evere wants to help, but for some reason the man desires to impress her. He finds her more and more beautiful every day and a strange crush begins to form in him. He thought he loved her before, but this time feels different.

He first tries to fish, but learns his hands are insufficient in holding onto slippery surfaces. A weapon will have to be obtained. Alphason remembers his story that led him up to this point. There are many things he will never forget. One memory, in particular, will prove to be useful at a time like this.

He returns to Evere and communicates to wait where she is, as he hands her the fur from Ghost. As long as the mountains are at his back, and the light from the fur points to Evere, he will be able to return. It is the rusted sword that was dropped when the New Word fled is what he is after.

One thing he does not consider is how he is going to retrace his steps to find the sword. Enthusiasm takes him over, as he does not care to worry about little problems such as this. He runs into what he believes is the direction only to become lost, as worry replaces his thoughts.

This moment of apprehension is brief, as he looks behind him and sees the mountains, along with the beacon from Evere. He settles at peace that he may not find the sword because at least he'll know his way back. The search for the weapon is not over as he continues his quest.

This could take forever, and an impatient Evere are the new thoughts he is considering. A trail will have to be picked up at some point to find the missing artifact, and it will have to be soon. He prays to the Word for guidance on top of a small rocky hill and believes the path will be shown.

A monster is coming he heard throughout the air. It is below him from whence it came. Standing on four legs at the bottom of the hill, a fully grown grizzly bear snarls, showing its long flesh-chewing teeth. Giants do not seem to exist anymore in their world, as the bear is at average height, but it is still too big for Alphason to underestimate it.

It begins charging up the hill to where he is as Alphason runs down the other way. It would have been a good time to use the dog's fur, as he wishes he had not given it to Evere. Now would have been a good time to use it. The quest turns into a chase across the land, as Alphason hopes the bear will tire before he does.

The chase takes him to the edge of a cliff, giving Alphason no more room to run. The bear already catches up to him before the man remembers where he is. This is the cliff that he had climbed up when he finally reunited with Evere and remembers that the sword was dropped near here. It is a place of reconciliation for him.

There is no time to reminisce about the miracle that had occurred here. The bear is running full force towards him, which pulls him out of his thoughts. He finally sees the sword the bear has just passed by on the ground. It will be a trick to somehow get passed the charging animal.

An idea quickly forms in him that if he waits here long enough the beast will lunge at him. If he steps out of the way at just the right moment, the bear will fall to his doom from the cliff. He waits for this moment, as he stands poised to jump.

The memories of this place break open inside his mind, again. A smile stretches on his face because he knows that the Word will not forsake him. Not here, of all places.

Things don't always turn out as they seem. When the bear comes within a leap of him, there is not a lunge. It halts and plunks down right in front of him. For some good reason, it begins licking a paw showing disinterest in the man it was chasing.

He takes this opportunity, while it is grooming and tip-toes around it towards the sword. When he picks it up, he walks back to the bear and raises the sword above it to strike. The bear does not move, or change its routine. It would be an easy glory for Alphason to take back this victory for Evere, but it doesn't seem right. He releases it from his burden of hunger, as he turns to make his trip back to Evere, with sword in hand.

Before his return, he detours towards a pond filled with fish who have never seen a fisherman before. A time has not come for the fish to fall for the bait at the end of a hook. It takes Alphason a few tries but succeeds at his new found talent. The sword proves to be useful to stab at slippery surfaces. It is still too slick for him to carry until he learns to use his coat to hold them.

The light brings him back to Evere, who seems to have been busy while he was away. Five fish were placed in front of where Evere is sitting on a log. He feels a little embarrassed, as he wanted to be the one to find food. "How did you manage to catch those?" he asks, as he sits down beside her.

He almost forgets she couldn't hear, as he begins writing his question in the ground. She shrugs, as she points toward the woods. A familiar roaring sound is in the air. The bear that had chased him trots out of the trees into the light. Ghost's fur does not have any effect on it.

A fish that is in its mouth drops by the other five. Alphason stands up to face the bear. "Now you listen here. Why do you come here? It was not your place to find those." The bear lumbers over to Evere, as it lays down on its back getting a relaxing rub by the woman on its belly. It grabs one of the fish with its paw, as it puts it into its mouth. "You go from being a slave to the New Word to being a slave for this bear. Unbelievable." It is a word he often uses.

He kneels in front of Evere and begins writing in the dirt, explaining to her that she will not be able to eat the fish raw, like the bear could. It is going to be a trick, considering he had never prepared a fish before. The bird is the only meat he's ever eaten.

First a fire needs to be built, as he gathers sticks around the area. The kindling is something he knows will burn, but he is without the knowledge on how to create the first spark. He prays again to the Word, hoping an idea will come to him. The day man discovers how to make fire is to come much later in human history, but a fire is going to be needed now. It is a time of miracles they are in at their present.

He piles all the sticks, lays rocks around in case the fire will spread, and places the sword on top, as he hopes history can possibly repeat itself. Another prayer is given, as he hopes the sword will ignite again.

It does not work, but another idea does form as he grabs the fur from Evere and tries to shed the light from it onto the sword. The light will not work either, as he becomes frustrated, turning his back on the sword.

He should have never turned his back. It would have been interesting to see the answered prayer that comes from a bolt of flame from the heavens, hitting the blade, as the metal of the old age relights. The fire engulfs the pile of sticks, and the rocks are sufficient in keeping it from spreading.

He wants to use the sword to peel the skin off of the fish but decides sharp rocks will have to do now that the sword carries fire again. His hands are used to remove the guts.

The prepared fish is brought to the fire, as he uses a stick to hold it over like he did with the bird. After enough time passes, the fish is ready, as he gives it to Evere. She places it in her mouth and lets it sit a little before she begins chewing. It actually does not make her gag. In fact, a smile forms on her face, as she begins to chew. She writes in the ground a message thanking him. Alphason feels good about this moment in his maturity. He finds he is getting somewhere with her.

After they have enough strength from the fish, the singer returns to the couple, whose bare feet can now be seen, standing next to the fire. The rest of him is still invisible. The feet begin running again, as Alphason grabs the sword that had burned out. They resume the chase that was postponed over two seasons. The fish they had eaten helps them to go further to keep up with the child, but eventually run out of energy again. The child does not wait for them.

Evere and Alphason stand before the mountains that had grown some but are still far away. They look at each other's eyes and wonder how they are to spend their time until the child shows up again. An idea does come eventually, but this next part will not be mentioned in the story, as privacy is expected for a man and a woman who become one flesh.

Nine months later a child is born. Winter had passed without a single snowflake on the ground since they left the point of no return. It is a boy. Evere and Alphason believe it is given to them by the Word, but it was not an easy delivery. No one knew exactly how to bring a child into this world. Something had happened during the birth that led to scars on Alphason's face, but peace has returned to the family.

The singer also returns. Half of his body is visible, and it seems that some kind of progress is being achieved. The half invisible child runs off again, but due to a newborn the family cannot keep up again. They decide to continue anyway to the mountains where they believe the child is going, but at their own pace.

Winter comes around again, within a day from reaching the mountains. Snow returns to the land. It is a welcome sight for the family, but worry grows in them as they wonder how they are going to survive. Alphason, whose hair had turned to full gray, as Evere's showed more streaks of silver in hers, remembers his survival skills he had learned when he was aided by Ghost. A cave will have to be found when they arrive.

One other loose end is at the foot of the mountains that is going to prove to be helpful during a long hard winter. Night has fallen, as a small multitude of twenty to thirty men in white robes are waiting for them. Evere and Alphason are cautious, for they look to be the fallen sand. Gloom are not on their faces, but inner warmth glows within them. They seem to be very pleased to greet the family that was only talked about in stories amongst them. Alphason takes out his fur to help illuminate the gathering.

"It has been too long old friend," speaks a voice, as the family stands in front of them. "We have been waiting for you."

CHAPTER 32

Psalm 119

Noel knelt in the snow before a cave, staring at the inner walls that reflected an orange wavy light. Heat was felt from where he was. A thick beard reaching down to the bottom of his neck had developed on his face. It was something that didn't start growing until he found the first of the chosen. Thin hairs began appearing on his scalp, as well and were something that was showing at a slower rate.

Flames could now be seen that had finally reached the surface, but everyone was a safe distance away. A crowd of twenty stood behind the scout that looked like followers. Their hands were free of paragons-of-past but were holding each other's arms in an expression of brotherly love. They agreed to be orderly and were standing from shortest to tallest to understand better the subtle differences between them.

"Is it time for us to look for the one we were led out here to find?" asked one standing in the center of the group. Even though he wasn't the tallest or shortest, he seemed to have the biggest nose and enjoyed a good mystery.

They wanted to be in high spirits for finally being unconstrained from the cave and the influence of the New Word, but they were sharing the mood held by the one that guided them out here. Noel displayed a character of someone who still held a burden. "The fire has separated us from the rest. This would be a good thing if it weren't for the fact that we are not all accounted for. I know they are still preserved. But with all my knowledge of this world, I still do not have the slightest clue as to where they could be going. The caves underneath are vast and could lead anywhere. I cannot give up in retrieving them."

"Can we form a plan?" An answer didn't come, as Noel rose on his feet and strode through the crowd. They separated to allow him room to walk through. A flat snowy field was behind them where a bird of wonder had fallen from a skirmish. They had witnessed some of the war that was going on in the sky between those with feathers. It looked more like a massacre than it was a battle.

Two wall-like cliffs were in the distance, and it seemed to be where Noel was heading at a quick pace. The others were hesitant in following, as they remembered the rule of covering their tracks, but it seemed their scout didn't care anymore. A change in emphasis had taken place as a different campaign was underway.

The first who was found by the scout was also the shortest of the group. He was the first to trust and was the first to follow in his rescuer's uncovered footsteps. The rest in orderly fashion followed behind the baby-faced member, as they ran to catch up.

When they reached the fallen bird, Noel chose to ignore it but some reached out their hands to touch what it was they feared so much. One near the back of the group, with a bloodhound look in his eyes, plucked a feather off and tucked it inside his robe.

The scout abruptly stopped, as he turned to the group. "We do not have to worry about these birds anymore. They were never really a threat to us, but the crow are still out there. They are not interested in us, but will be without a purpose when the rest of the white feathers are killed off. In order to exist, they will try and find any reason to keep their purpose alive. Do not take anything from this slain bird, or you may suffer the consequences."

The one with the bloodhound eyes took his words to heart, as he nervously retrieved the feather out from his robe. Everyone saw him this time as he coyly dropped it onto the ground. "Did these birds have a name?" he asks, hoping it would distract the others from what he just did.

"Evere gave it one, though she may not remember. She thought she was dreaming when she first encountered it, though it was a smaller version. Unfortunately, it was something she never shared for others to hear. The Word knows its name, but answers in what you seek are not found here. We must keep moving."

Noel set the line in hurried motion again, as he continued towards a path through the cliffs. It didn't take long, as they reached the other side where they got a wider look at a bigger world around them. They halted once more to take it all in. More mountains and trees were spread out throughout the land, but this was not what they were marveling at. Two lights from opposite directions could be seen by all. One from the left was a softer light that glowed over the horizon. The other from the right was an intense pillar that was beaming to the top of the sky.

"Here's the design," proposed Noel. "Let's say one way leads to Alphason. It is the end result we are all looking for with a value on efficiency. The other way leads to the rest of the chosen. It may take longer, but will give us a more fulfilling conclusion. What do you all think is the better way?"

"How do we know which way will actually lead to the others?" questioned a tall one that was standing right behind him. He was unaware how loud his voice was through the ears of Noel. It caused his leader to cringe.

"We do not know for sure, but we can know what it is we really want."

"I want to be a champion, just like you!" Noel turned to the one that spoke.

"For now on, you shall be known as the one who shouts. Which way do you think is our brethren?"

"I believe the Old Word guides our paths. He will show us the way. Maybe this is the reason why the one on the right is clearer to see. The Word is like a lamp unto our feet and a light to our path. We hide the truth in our hearts so that we may never lose our way again."

"Someone should be writing this all down. Your words carry the weight of a scroll."

"What is a scroll?"

"You'll see someday. Shall we all continue?" Their run commenced, setting their course towards the beacon, keeping a uniformity intact.

Noel's mood changed again. He was in a cheerful humor and was infectious to the ones behind him.

**

Even though the light beam was very clear to see, it was quite a distance for the remnant. Their fascination never faded from their endeavor to reach it. Hours passed before they finally caught a glimpse of a small mountain it was purging from. The mount looked like an egg that had cracked open as everyone halted to examine it.

"We will have to find a way on top," suspected Noel.

"How are we to accomplish this?" asked the tall one, with the old man's face, who was also the first to be found by the scout. He wasn't as quick to trust as some but was losing doubt by the minute.

"I saw a cave painting that showed a dog with an uncanny ability to fly."

"You expect us to fly?"

"He didn't undertake this on his own. He had help."

"From who?"

"A giant stepped in. A glowing ball proved to be useful, as well."

"And where is our giant?"

"Our giant is us. There is a ledge I can see from here. If we shoulder each other's weight, one on top of the other, we can reach it."

"Where do we go if we reach this ledge?"

"It is too high to see, but if we make it, we will see then what our next step should be."

A pyramid was the plan. They had to rearrange themselves to make it work. The strongest weren't necessarily the tallest, but they ordered themselves accordingly. Twenty was just enough to make it on top but only a few were able to climb onto the narrow shelf. Noel was not one of them that made it.

"Where do we go from here?" wondered the baby-face who was one of the five. He looked further up the mountain to see the progress they made. "It looks like we are only a fraction of the way there."

They didn't notice it until now. Even though five climbed to the ledge, a sixth one was sprawled out on it with them. He was darker-skinned and looked to be dead or passed out.

"We found one." The baby-face looked down towards the rest who didn't make it. "How are we going to bring Noel up here?"

"He was one of the stronger ones," answered a skinny one with a bushy unibrow. "He was on the bottom, creating a base. The better question is how are we going to get down?"

The baby-face carefully stepped over the others to examine the body that was lying up here with them. His hands were the first thing he observed. There was nothing in them. After a light tap on the cheek, the free survivor woke. "The wind has them."

"You speak of the wind," responded the baby-face, trying to understand. "Explain yourself."

"Most fell down. Some were taken away by bats. Others were raptured."

"I don't understand." The wind around them began picking up almost blowing them off the edge.

"A giant opened the earth to receive them. They were caught up in a great storm." The survivor began pointing behind the baby-face towards the night sky. "He will know." Noel was hovering high in the air. His robe was flapping in a wind that seemed to be under his control. A gust began pushing him towards the ledge, as everyone on the side of the mountain and the ground were mesmerized.

"How can this be?" shouted the baby-face at Noel, who was gently placed onto the ledge with them.

"My place is coming back to me," answered Noel. "I didn't know how to master this element before until now. All of you will be able to do the things that I can do someday, but not until we find Alphason first. Your weight will not be a problem for me in bringing you all down from here. I see you found a survivor."

"We did. He has told us a strange tale of a giant and a powerful wind, but I see now that it may not be too hard to swallow."

"I know this giant. He is one of us, but he had a slightly different perspective in all of this." Noel knelt down to the survivor for some of his own questions. "Where did the rest go?"

"I do not know, but I was left behind to tell their story. There is no reason to go any further. I am the only one that is left."

"This is good news you have for me." The weakened one reached up to grab his arms.

"Listen to what I have to tell you! The New Word has fallen. He has led many to a dark place."

"I am informed of this. You are in good company, my friend. Come with us. There is a path to take that is set for you, and I believe there is a place where we will all meet. The ones that were taken away by the wind may have a head start, but we will have to catch up."

"Maybe we should have gone the other way towards Alphason?" questioned the baby-face, who was standing over them. "It seems we have missed them."

"We chose our path. It is best to commit to it. If one was all we were able to find, then all of this was worth it."

"Which way are we to go? There are no more beacons of light to follow."

"You are wrong in this. There is another way yet to follow. None of you are able to see it like me. It is a light I have been following ever since I have met Alphason, and it has been growing brighter every day."

"You'll have to take us there if you are the only one who sees it."

"Not to worry. My time with all of you isn't over yet."

**

From tallest to shortest, everyone followed in single-file behind Noel. The pace was still in a hastened walk. They were crossing over a land, whose snow was melting. Mud was being tracked onto their white robes, but none of them seemed to mind. Enough trees were in the region, they felt as if they were passing through a forest.

The baby-face was right behind the leader and had some thoughts that were unanswered. "Can you describe this light that you are seeing?"

"It may be a challenge to explain." A climb up a steep hill began as they conversed. "It is a light that has been growing but is like a land that I haven't stepped into yet. It is getting to a point that the light will blind me if I do not enter into it."

"What is keeping you from doing this?"

"I fear that if I do, then I will not be with you all any longer."

"How will we find Alphason if that were to happen?"

"I believe that this light leads me to my purpose. It will lead us to Alphason, and when that happens then you all will have no more need for a scout such as myself."

It seemed like a day had surfaced at Noel's feet. When they reached the top of the hill, a blinding light was swallowing them up. No one seemed affected, except for Noel, who was forced to keep his eyes closed.

"Where did he go!?" shouted the one-who-shouts from the back of the line. Everyone in the group looked to be missing something. Noel turned around as he opened his eyes to a group who were becoming unhinged.

"What has you all bewildered?"

"I hear his voice."

"Is the light blinding you all, as well?"

"There is no light that we can perceive," answered the baby-face, "but it seems we have somehow misplaced your body. We can still hear you, however?"

"What can you see?"

"Mountains. I see the others. They look to be resting in a soft pasture near the foot."

"This is something that even I cannot see. The light around me prevents me from comprehending past it."

"It must mean something."

"It means we have arrived. This is where we will all meet. The rest of the chosen are nearby, and Alphason will be here shortly. If he has succeeded in achieving his own personal goals, he will have company with him, as well. Think of all the time that has passed to reach this moment. A little more patience may be needed, but it will be worth the passing. The anticipation cannot be greater."

CHAPTER 33

The Gathering

"We have been waiting for you." The family had finally reached the mountains that had been within their vision for two long years. There was much ground to cover besides the distance that was needed to touch this place. A language was learned and a family had taken root. Fear was confronted and new levels of faith had been achieved.

One thing that hasn't changed is the fact that Evere still can't hear anything. Alphason scans the many faces smiling at them. He can't fathom who it is that is speaking. "You'll have to excuse my wife. It has been a long time since her ears had worked, and I was told by someone that I was going blind. Who is it that speaks to me?"

"You are not going blind. In fact, you are able to see more than ever before. In ten short years, you will be ready to take your second glance into eternity." Alphason continues studying the crowd to identify who it is that is talking, but no one's lips are moving.

"Your voice sounds somewhat familiar."

"You have an excellent memory. It had to have been over a hundred years since you have heard my voice."

"If it is the one that we found in the river then why is it I cannot see you?"

"I'm standing right in front of you, Alphason. You cannot see me anymore until your eyes into eternity open up within you. Before that is to happen, you will have to leave your body indefinitely. The same goes for Evere. She will survive a little longer than you. When it is her time, being able to hear again will be just a taste of the wonders that wait for you on the other side."

"Do you know of the child that has led us out here?"

"I do. He's standing right behind you. Careful, it may be frightening at first." When Alphason turns around, the singer is standing where his shadow would have been. Evere sees him too, as she covers her mouth to keep from screaming. His whole body can be seen except for his eyes. The ground on the other side of him can be viewed through where his eyes should have been. It is a frightening revelation, but Alphason understands it now.

"When these ten years are over. I will be able to see what he sees."

"Child-Like Faith is his name. It is a depressing thought for the fallen sand. For you, it is your link to the Word." Alphason turns back around, as he watches the child run into the mountains, but there is more to be understood at this meeting.

"Why are all these people here? They seem to want something from me."

"You helped me to remember my name. They would like to know theirs."

"I don't understand."

"We are known as the Light Bearers of the Hidden Word, who are in waiting to be restored by the man that was created by the Word. Our relationship with the Word was never cut. It was just lengthened to chronicle where the Word is taking us seen from the footstool of earth. My memory and my place have come back to me, which is why you are unable to see me with your faulty eyes. They, however, are in waiting to begin their journey to find their place again. It all begins with a word from you."

"I do not know what it is you want me to say."

"You already said it. They just needed to hear your voice. You do not realize this, but your voice sounds exactly like the Word's voice. Your laugh sounds like His laugh. He gave you a similar one, so it would trigger their memories from the time they were with Him. Not only that, but he also has given you his likeness."

"Unbelievable."

"You will learn to stop saying that. At some point, you will believe everything you see."

"We must be moving on. We have a family now, and it is growing very cold."

"There is a cave near here. They will take you to it, but they were hoping to continue their visit with you a little longer. There are so many stories they would like to share with you before you pass on. Starting with their names."

"Are you not staying?"

"My time has come to an end. It was my purpose to hear the news first and bring them to you. My job is done. I will go now to the place I was before I entered the river. Thank you, Alphason, for what you did for me."

"It is the Word that made it possible. Not me. When will you go?" His silence gave him is answer.

The rest of the Light Bearers urge him and his family with them to the cave. One thought is nagging on his mind while they walk. "I never got his name." It is a question among many that would carry on throughout the generations. Many of which that would remain without answers until the end of time, or the beginning of eternity.

EPILOGUE

The Sleeper Wakes

Back at The Wisdom Tree, the sleeper is gazing around him at the grand view encompassing him from the hill. He had just woken up from a long rest. It is the evening, and it feels good being up here. The warm breeze would keep any weary traveler from wanting to leave.

Something is bothering him, as he searches the hill he is on top of, leaving no stone or long blade of grass unturned. The sleeper is a man of no extraordinary features about him, other than feet that only has one black shoe on them. He has short hair with a part on the left side but looks like it could have used some grooming on a lightly tanned face. His dark blue t-shirt and khaki pants seems to have been torn to go along with his dirty blonde messy hair. "Where is my shoe at? I could have sworn I heard a voice around here. Whoever you are, if you seem to know where my shoe is, I would appreciate that you return it."

"Have you lost something?" asks a deep voice that sounded like it came from the top of the tree. The man tries to see where the voice is coming from, but he cannot see past the limbs that are too high for him to climb.

"You know what I lost."

"May I ask you a question? Can you remember why you need the shoe, or anything about your life before you woke up here?" The man looks down at his feet, as he tries to comprehend the question. He realizes that this tree is the first thing he can remember. For some reason he knows he wants the shoe but can't remember why. He can't even recall his name.

"You seem to know more about me than I know myself, which is probably why you are up there and I'm down here."

"I am here to help you through this. A lot has become of you, but you will not be allowed to know exactly what happened that led you to here. You will have to move on without this knowledge. It is best that you don't remember. The future is all that matters here at the Wisdom Tree."

"Did I die?"

"It is the first question to be answered. Your life here was preceded by your death, yes. The world you see around you, however, is still alive but plagued with problems. Wars are raging. It is one war really. Armageddon is its name. The end of all of it will be coming soon, but you will be kept safe here, as you wait for what is promised to you. A long time ago you put your trust into a king that made it possible for you to be here. This tree you are at will be the last thing you will remember about a troubled earth. Patience is needed before we can carry on before this age comes to an end. Stories will be helpful in passing the time."

"I thought I heard you telling a story when I woke up, but I only caught the end of it. Will you share me that one?"

"Of course. In fact, it has much in common with where you are at right now. It is a story about trees. There are many more stories to come after. There are others here that you do not see, but they have already heard this one. They are in waiting to hear about a world war, but the hourglass will be turned on its head one more time for those who have not heard. It all begins with the Word."

About the Author

Springfield, Missouri is where Jonathan Hammock keeps his stuff. Nicaragua is where God would like him to go. He has been there three times for missions and always comes home fulfilled but unsatisfied, because there is still so much more life to live, and it cannot be wasted. Home is a place that God is providing for him, but it will be at the end of a long journey. This is his first book, but he has many planned.

Printed in the United States
By Bookmasters